sunfall

Praise for the *everafter* series

ForeWord Reviews 2009 Book of the Year Awards Finalist for Horror

everafter

"Stark and Tam have managed to scare the bejesus out of me in their highly skilled effort to introduce Valentine and Alexa, two professional students, who are thrust into the forbidden realm of Vampires and Weres. ...the writing is superb, the characters believable, the plot strong...I have to give these authors kudos."
—*Kissed By Venus*

nevermore

"You will not be able to put this book down once you start. I found it well written and totally interesting and I recommend it to any of you who are interested in the shifter concept."—Amos Lassen, *Literary Pride*

What reviewers say about Nell Stark's fiction

Visit us at www.boldstrokesbooks.com

By Nell Stark and Trinity Tam

everafter

nevermore

nightrise

sunfall

By Nell Stark

Running With the Wind

Homecoming

sunfall

by

Nell Stark and Trinity Tam

2012

SUNFALL

ISBN 10: 1-60282-661-7
ISBN 13: 978-1-60282-661-8

THIS TRADE PAPERBACK ORIGINAL IS PUBLISHED BY
BOLD STROKES BOOKS, INC.
P.O. BOX 249
VALLEY FALLS, NY 12185

FIRST EDITION: MAY 2012

CREDITS
EDITOR: CINDY CRESAP
PRODUCTION DESIGN: SUSAN RAMUNDO
COVER DESIGN BY SHERI (GRAPHICARTIST2020@HOTMAIL.COM)

Acknowledgments

For the last four years, we have shared our lives with Valentine Darrow and Alexa Newland. While mostly amenable roommates, they have been at times stubborn and demanding. They have dictated how we spent our summer vacations and what time we went to bed at night. They have caused more than a few arguments between us. They have also inspired some rather passionate "apologizing."

We thought it would be bittersweet to bring Val and Alexa's story to a close, but really, nothing has changed. They are still here, sipping chai at the corner Starbucks and jogging the pre-dawn streets of the East Village. Every new park and restaurant and curio shop we encounter in New York City inevitably inspires a conversation about whether or not it might be one of Alexa and Val's haunts. They've wormed their way into our world and we're grateful that you have invited them into yours.

As we close the book on Val and Alexa's adventures, we are first and foremost grateful to Cindy Cresap, who has helped us to weave together the many threads of their story.

We are likewise indebted to Radclyffe for sowing the seed of this idea years ago, for her invaluable feedback on this narrative, and for giving us the opportunity to publish with Bold Strokes Books. We'd like to thank all of the wonderful, hardworking, and selfless people at BSB—Connie, Lori, Lee, Jennifer, Paula, Sheri, and others—for helping to put out and market quality product year after year. The members of Team BSB, including our many fellow authors, continue to inspire us and we count you all in our extended family.

Finally, our thanks go out to each reader who picks up one of our books. This series is, above all, for you, and we hope you enjoy it.

Dedication

For Radclyffe—the Blood Prime of Clan BSB

alexa

CHAPTER ONE

The War Room was in chaos, and I took comfort in the light pressure of Valentine's hand at the small of my back as we entered. Crimson alarm lights flickered dramatically, and the digital marquee winding around the room proclaimed a state of "Code Red." People either were milling about aimlessly or were huddled together in small groups, and the air hummed with their cumulative whispers. They darted frequent glances toward the large plasma screens that covered the walls, all of which were focused on one image: the starkly imposing façade of the front entrance to the New York City Four Seasons.

In a matter of hours, Helen Lambros, Master vampire of New York, would walk to her death through that door. On the other side waited Balthasar Brenner, a powerful alpha werewolf who had vowed to destroy the vampire/wereshifter Consortium. Brenner was holding an entire delegation of vampires hostage, and his price for their release was Helen's surrender. He had already declared his intent to imprison her in the penthouse suite and watch her die as the sun rose.

Brenner's vendetta against vampires had been centuries in the making. He considered them to be evolutionarily inferior to both humans and Weres, and his mission was simple: genocide. He had almost eradicated the bloodline of the Missionary, one of the seven great vampire clans, and the one to which Val belonged. For weeks, before she'd begun turning others, she had been the only surviving member and had claimed the titles of both Missionary and blood prime by default. Brenner had made three separate attempts on her life during that time, but she had always managed to foil him.

It was no surprise that Brenner despised the Consortium, an alliance specifically designed to help both species work together toward common aims. As far as he was concerned, wereshifters and vampires had no common aims. Every shifter who associated with the Consortium was, by his reckoning, a traitor. Now he was trying to make a powerful statement by forcing Helen, the Master of New York and head of the Order of Mithras, to go willingly to her own death.

If his plan succeeded, he would be able to claim credit for dispatching both the Were and vampire leaders of the most important Consortium base on the East Coast. Last month, Malcolm Blakeslee, Weremaster of New York, had been shot in the head by one of Brenner's assassins. He had spent several days in a coma before suddenly shifting. Initially, the doctors had taken his transformation as a good sign—a necessary part of his healing process. But for weeks, he had been living in the arena as a lion and many feared he had gone feral. In his absence, his assistant and my good friend, Karma Rao, had taken over his duties.

"There's Constantine." Val pointed to the glass walls of the small conference area across the room. Within, Constantine Bellande, the werepanther who had sired me, was locked in a heated debate with Leon Summers, the Consortium's head intelligence officer. Even at a distance, I could make out the flush that suffused Constantine's face and neck.

"Let's find out why they look so murderous." I led the way, noticing several stares directed toward Val as we crossed the floor. Had it not been for Brenner's deadly ultimatum, Valentine Darrow's miraculous return to the sunlight would have been the news monopolizing the rumor mill.

After Val had been turned almost two years ago, I had chosen to become a shifter in order to sustain her forever. Not only were Valentine and I deeply in love, we were also attuned to each other at the deep chemical level. For her, my blood was special. The vampire parasite that had colonized Val's bloodstream recognized my red cells as a substitute for her own, and so long as I was the only one who fed her, she would retain her soul and the ability to endure the sun. Unfortunately, thanks to Brenner, a wereshifter civil war had broken out while I'd been traveling in Africa over the summer, and I hadn't been able to return to Valentine as planned. She had lost control, and the Consortium physicians had given her a transfusion. Thus began her descent into darkness, and for several agonizing months, I had believed her to be lost to me forever. But then, the discovery of an ancient myth had rekindled my hope that Val could recover. After traveling to Argentina and tracking down a legendary plant with miraculous healing powers, I had been able to restore her soul.

· I reached for her hand and she squeezed gently in reassurance. We'd had less than a day together before Brenner's ultimatum had plunged the Consortium into bedlam. Part of me wanted to turn around and leave—to escape the city, drive into the mountains, and seclude ourselves in a cozy cabin where we could rediscover each other slowly and thoroughly. But a week of languid lovemaking was a luxury we'd have to indulge in after we solved this latest crisis.

When I pushed open the conference room doors, both men turned to regard me with angry expressions. My inner panther growled in response, but I refused to let her distress show on my face. "Problem, gentlemen?"

"Just a friendly disagreement about methodology." Constantine's voice was taut, the air around him fairly shimmering with tension. He was close to shifting, and I wondered how much of his volatility had to do with his personal feelings about Helen Lambros. I'd always suspected him of being at least a little in love with her, and now she was about to walk into a death trap with her eyes open. Moreover, she had just been reunited with a former lover, Solana Carrizo, whom she had believed to be dead for the past century. If my suspicions were correct, Constantine had multiple reasons for being on edge.

At that moment, Devon Foster, the vampire head of Consortium security, barged through the doors. "She's planning to leave in five hours. That doesn't give us much time."

Val braced her arms on the table. "Run us through how the exchange will work. Will Brenner release the hostages when she arrives?"

"'Once she's in custody,' were his exact words."

Val grimaced. "That phrase is a semantic minefield."

I slid into the chair closest to her. "We'll need two plans: one for extracting the hostages if Brenner doesn't let them go and the other purely focused on Helen."

"If he doesn't release the delegation," said Constantine, "his terms are forfeit and we have every right to go in and take them. And Helen."

"His terms have nothing to do with this," countered Summers. "That hotel is full of humans, and we'll almost certainly be apprehended by their law enforcement if we turn it into a war zone."

Constantine snarled in frustration. "Who said anything about a war zone? Alexa is right. This is an extraction mission. It will have to be surgically precise to have any hope of success."

"Whatever we decide, we need a backup plan." Val's fingers drummed a quick beat against the tabletop. "Is there a building with line-of-sight into the eastern wing of the penthouse that's also within sniper range?"

Foster's eyes narrowed. "What are you thinking?"

"A sniper gives us two options: the ability to create a distraction and to perform a mercy killing if necessary."

Constantine swore colorfully in French, but no one disagreed with Val's assessment of the possibilities. I tried to put myself in Helen's place. As a Sunrunner vampire, she could withstand direct exposure to the sunlight for much longer than members of the other vampire clans. But in the end, she would still be burned alive, her increased resistance only serving to prolong what was undoubtedly an agonizing process. A shiver coursed down my spine as I imagined her slow immolation. I would want the quick death Val was offering.

Summers was speaking into his phone, directing one of his staff members to find out whether there was a building that met Val's specifications. At a light tap on the door, Foster opened it to reveal one of her staff carrying a large roll of paper.

"Hotel schematics," Foster said as she spread out the blueprints. For several minutes, we contemplated them in silence.

"We'll have to find a way in through the service entrance." Constantine traced a set of parallel lines with his index finger. "From there, we can split into two teams, one creating a distraction in the elevator shaft while the other ascends the stairwell."

Summers's upper lip curled in disdain. "In what universe would Brenner leave the back door unguarded?"

Constantine's knuckles whitened and the table creaked at the strength of his grip. "I'm well aware that—"

"We can stow away on a delivery truck," I cut in, hoping to diffuse the tension by keeping them focused on the plan. "At least we'll make it through the perimeter that way."

For one harrowing moment, it looked as though they would come to blows despite my efforts. But then Summers's phone rang, and he stalked toward the back of the room as he answered it. I turned my attention back to the others.

"You and Leon should be in the elevator shaft," Val said, looking at Foster. "No windows."

"That leaves Constantine and me to cover the stairwell." I bent closer to inspect that part of the diagram.

A frown creased Val's brow. "And me. And Solana, if she's willing."

Val thought I had forgotten about her. I rested my palm atop hers and stroked her knuckles with my fingertips. "You need to be the sniper."

"What?"

That single syllable vibrated with tension. I took hold of her hand and pulled her into the corner, not wanting everyone else to be privy to our conversation. Val was reacting not as the blood prime or the Missionary, but as my lover, and I would need to respond to her as such. When we reached the far corner, I twined my arms around her neck and met the full force of her stormy gaze.

"I'm not leaving your side, Alexa," she said before I could open my mouth. "You just brought me back. Brought *us* back. This mission verges on suicidal, and if you think I'm going to sit around and twiddle my thumbs while you risk your life—"

I cut off her tirade by pressing my mouth to hers. I meant the kiss to be gentle and comforting, but the sensation of her lips sliding possessively over mine fanned the embers of my desire. A groan welled up in my throat, and I twined my fingers in the short hairs at the back of her neck. When she finally pulled away, we were both gasping for breath.

"Don't you see?" she whispered.

"Perfectly." I managed a small smile. "But you know I'm right about this. You should take the shot. When you're at full strength, your eyesight and muscle control are unparalleled. And the sunrise isn't a death sentence for you anymore."

Her eyes narrowed. "That's true of Solana, too."

"Solana would never be able to pull the trigger."

Her lean frame shuddered in a sigh, and I knew logic had won out. She pulled me closer, cradling my head against her shoulder, and gently stroked my hair. I let my eyes drift shut and savored the sensation of being held. Valentine's arms were the eye of the storm.

"Solana goes with you and Constantine," Val murmured into my ear. "I trust her, and you'll need someone at your back who can handle a weapon if you both end up having to shift."

I nodded against her chest and was about to reply when Summers's raised voice captured my attention.

"The thirty-eighth floor? You're sure? Good." An edge of anticipation had sharpened his words, and I reluctantly pulled away from Val to hear his news.

"Who's doing the shooting?" he said.

"I am." Val cast a sideways glance at me. "Under duress."

Summers bared his sharpened teeth. "My people found you a perch on the top floor of the Seagram Building. The angle of correspondence is small, but it's the only option."

"I'll make it work." Val squeezed my shoulders briefly before moving away to confer with him.

Constantine stepped into the space she had vacated, and my panther snapped awake as though he had called her name. His unspoken desire to grind Brenner's spine between his powerful teeth was both palpable and infectious, and a rush of adrenaline flooded my bloodstream. The remembered stench of urine and wet fur assailed my nose as I flashed back to our imprisonment at Brenner's hands. He had intended for Constantine and me to kill each other in captivity. He had unleashed a deadly virus on the shifters of New York. He had razed the vampire city of Sybaris, and his assassins had made three separate attempts on Valentine's life. He had much to answer for, and we would make him pay.

The hunt was on.

CHAPTER TWO

We gathered at half past three in the morning in a small atrium just off the back door of Headquarters, a restricted area that had required Foster's handprint to access. From here, we could leave on our mission without risking the speculation of passers-by. Brenner undoubtedly had spies inside the Consortium, and while he had to suspect the existence of some kind of rescue attempt for Helen, we needed to keep the specifics of our plan under tight wraps.

Just minutes before, the bedraggled contingent of Sunrunners had been released to us outside of Wilmington, Delaware. Brenner had left them chained inside a camper trailer by an RV park. Only an hour before, he had sent a terse communiqué with their coordinates. Summers had made the arrangements with the Philadelphia branch of the Consortium to pick them up. We had anxiously watched their recovery on a secure satellite feed, half expecting some kind of ambush. The extraction team had been forced to cut things closer than they'd like, what with sunrise being only a few hours off, but ultimately all of the delegates were collected and accounted for. They appeared healthy, if malnourished, aside from their leader, Bai. Second-in-command to Tian, the Blood Prime of the Sunrunners, Bai had been wheeled in with his neck immobilized in a brace. The Consortium rescue squad had found him unconscious and badly beaten. When the other delegates were questioned, they revealed that they had been held separately and had no idea how or why Bai had been tortured. Val had wanted him to be transported here, but Constantine had overruled her, arguing that until we had neutralized Brenner's threat, all of New York City should be considered a hot zone.

The hostages' return had allowed us to shift our focus entirely to Helen's rescue. We had already been over the tactics dozens of times in hastily rendered computer simulations, and we were as ready to go as time would allow. The members of our small group were dressed entirely in black, and all of us were armed to the teeth. Just moments ago, I had watched Valentine strap two semiautomatic pistols to her belt and slide a knife into her ankle sheath. Now, she was crouching over her sniper rifle, inspecting it for the second time tonight. She bent to make an adjustment, and desire stirred in me at the sight of her strong, elegant fingers moving over the bones of the firearm. When a strand of golden hair slipped into her eyes, I knelt beside her and smoothed the errant lock away from her face.

She leaned into my touch and smiled. "You're breathtaking."

"Oh? You find the commando look attractive?"

A grin played at the corners of her mouth. "I love when you go commando, baby."

"You have a teenage boy's sense of humor." I rolled my eyes for her benefit, secretly glad she felt capable of humor despite the thick tension in the room.

My attention was suddenly drawn to Foster moving toward the inner door, her cell phone pressed to her ear. She opened the door to admit Solana. This was the first time I'd ever seen Solana with her dark hair pulled back, and the look accentuated the sharpness of her cheekbones. A slight redness lingered around her eyes, but otherwise, she betrayed no sign of internal distress. Her reunion with Helen had been a century in the making, but they'd had only a few hours together before Brenner's ultimatum had turned the entire Consortium on its head.

I stepped forward to fold my arms around her, but her posture remained stiff despite my embrace. I could empathize; her heart was shattering, and to let her guard down even for an instant would spell the disintegration of her composure.

"Tell me what I've missed," was all she said.

I stepped back and motioned to Constantine. "Have you met?"

Solana inclined her head as he joined us. "Earlier this evening."

Constantine kept his hands clasped behind his back. When he spoke, his tone was cool. "You'll be joining us as we make our way up the stairwell. We expect heavy resistance, and it's safe to assume that Alexa and I will be four-footed for much of the mission, as will Brenner's forces. Have you fought against Weres before?"

"I have not."

"Aim for the head. We can recover from almost anything else."

"I'll need weapons."

I pointed to the far corner where an open duffle bag fairly bristled with side arms. "Take whatever you need."

"The truck's ETA is fifteen minutes," called Summers, whose operatives had commandeered a produce freighter bound for the Four Seasons.

A wave of anxiety prickled beneath my skin, and suddenly, I couldn't bear the space separating me from Valentine. She glanced up as I approached, and my face must have betrayed some hint of my inner turmoil because she immediately got to her feet. When her arms came around my waist, I laid my head on her chest. Her heartbeat pulsed against my cheek, and I let its rhythm steady my nerves.

Her heartbeat. It had been many hours since she'd last tasted my blood, and she needed to be at her sharpest and strongest for this mission. Besides, I craved the intimacy of her teeth in my vein—the knowledge that I was nourishing her, empowering her, satisfying her. I pulled back just enough to tug the collar of my shirt down over my left shoulder.

"Drink me."

Val jerked as if I'd struck her. Darkness swallowed her sparkling blue irises at my command. She struggled to rein in her thirst, but I cupped the back of her neck with one hand.

"Don't think. Don't hesitate. I want you, and you need this. Feed, my love."

The last band of her restraint snapped, and she crushed my body to hers. I swallowed a moan as her teeth pierced me, pain and pleasure fusing in every cell. Desperate to feel her skin against mine, I pushed my free hand beneath the hem of her sweater and skimmed my knuckles along the taut muscles of her abdomen. Everyone could hear her muffled groan, but I didn't care.

In another minute, I might have begged her to take me, regardless of our audience. But before I could speak the words, she wrenched herself away, shuddering. The tendons in her forearms leapt into sharp relief above clenched fists, and her dilated eyes never left mine as she battled for control. My panther prowled restlessly behind the doors of my brain, craving the satisfaction she'd been denied. Beyond words, I sucked in one deep breath after another, torn between animal desires and human reason.

Val finally closed the gap between us. Her feeding frenzy had passed like a summer thunderstorm. Her hands were gentle as they clasped my shoulders, and her mouth moved tenderly over the bite mark as she cleaned the fading puncture wounds with delicate strokes of her tongue.

"Thank you." She murmured the words against the shell of my ear, so softly as to almost be inaudible. "I love you."

I cupped her face in my hands. "We have unfinished business. After this is over, I plan to finish it. So come back to me."

"Baby." Her mouth twisted in a lopsided smile. "I'll be light years from the action. You're the one riding into the heart of the storm."

"Truck's here," Summers called.

A hush fell over the group, and I was able to make out the spitting sound of gravel against asphalt as overburdened tires neared the door. As we filed out into the night and climbed into the shipping container, the scent of garlic enveloped us.

"Good thing that particular allergy is misinformation," Val said dryly.

Foster wrinkled her nose. "At least our scent will be masked if Brenner has his dogs at the loading dock."

I settled onto the floor with my back against a crate, and Val joined me as the truck began to move. The muscles in her thigh were tight beneath my hand as I stroked her gently, needing the connection.

"All right, people." Summers raised his voice over the creaking of the axles. "This mission is going to get ugly fast. We'll need to cut communications early on to avoid tipping Brenner off to our location. Val, if you don't hear from us by sunrise, take your shot. We clear?"

"Crystal." Val covered my hand with her own, lacing our fingers together. When I tried to meet her eyes, I found her locked in some kind of staring contest with Solana, who nodded almost imperceptibly before looking away.

"What's going on?" I asked, trying to keep my tone light.

But before she could answer, the truck made a sharp turn and lurched to a halt. "Seagram Building." The driver's words came disembodied into my ear bud.

"This is my stop." Val brushed her knuckles against my cheek with the lightness of a butterfly's wing, but her eyes were bright and fierce. "Don't show them any mercy."

Again, the visceral memory of my captivity by Brenner overwhelmed me: the pungent stench of rot and urine and desperation mingled with the fear that Constantine and I would turn on each other before we could escape.

I shook my head to free myself of the flashback. "Believe me, I won't."

Despite the agitation I could read in the taut lines of her face, Val's kiss was tender. "I love you."

"I know. I'll see you soon."

With that, she was gone.

As the truck accelerated, I leaned my head back against the crate and closed my eyes, unwilling to betray to the others just how difficult it was to be separated from her. Once Brenner's threat was neutralized, I would see to it that we left town for a while. We needed time alone to learn each other anew. Ever since Val had been turned into a vampire, our relationship had been a protracted battle against the odds. We had persisted in the face of obstacles others had called insurmountable: her thirst, my panther, my illness, her descent into darkness. After so much conflict, we needed the chance to take a deep breath together. I wanted to lie in her arms for hours—to bask in the sight and scent and taste of her without pressing agendas or the threat of emergency.

A sudden presence where Val had been snapped me out of my reverie, and I opened my eyes to the sight of Solana settling in beside me.

"How are you?" she asked, her voice warm with empathy.

I felt selfish for being on the receiving end of her comfort. My lover would be far from the center of action, but hers was Brenner's target.

"I think you know. Let's talk about something else."

"Gladly."

"What was that little exchange you had with Val, hmm?"

The hint of a smile curved Solana's lips. "She wanted me to watch your back."

"Oh? So you're a mind reader now?"

"I didn't have to read her mind to know exactly what she was thinking."

"We're all going to get through this," I said, channeling a confidence I wanted to feel. "Every single one of us."

Again, the truck slowed dramatically. As it began to turn, the driver's voice echoed in my head. "ETA, one minute."

"Roger." Summers got to his feet. "Val, do you read?"

"Loud and clear." Relief swept through me at the sound of her strong, albeit breathless, voice.

"Any problems so far?"

"Nothing I can't handle."

"Good. We're going to black for our approach."

"Got it. Stay safe. Especially you, Panthro."

I smiled at the memory of the first time she'd used that nickname—nearly two years ago now on a brief vacation in the Catskills where I'd finally had a breakthrough in successfully handling my panther. But now was not the time for a trip down memory lane. Shaking off the nostalgia, I rose to a crouch and thumbed off the safety on my pistol as Foster picked her way toward the sliding metal door. After the driver opened it, she would have only a moment in which to neutralize any obvious threat. I was hoping Brenner's foot soldiers wouldn't be lying in wait, but luck hadn't exactly been on our side thus far.

I steadied myself against the crate as the truck lurched into a three-point turn. The driver cut the engine and opened his door, and I prepared for the beginning of a firefight. But when he began to whistle "You Are My Sunshine" under his breath, I felt a glimmer of hope. That was his all-clear signal. Was it possible that Brenner hadn't deployed anyone to guard the service entrance? Had he underestimated our resourcefulness, or did he think the Consortium believed Helen to be dispensable?

The door grated harshly as its ball bearings slid along the rusty tracks. A gust of cold air rushed into the container, and my panther pushed for control. She wanted out of this box just as much as I did. Soon, I would have no reason to resist her, but for now two legs would serve me better than four.

"Clear," Foster whispered, sounding incredulous. One by one, we stepped out onto the smooth cement of the garage. Aside from several dollies leaned up against the wall and a Dumpster in the far corner, it was empty.

"Where the fuck are they?" muttered Summers.

I didn't want to look a gift horse in the mouth, but I couldn't help sharing his cynicism. And then, as though he had issued a summons, a female security officer stepped out of a door to our left. She was squinting at something in her palm—a phone, probably—and didn't immediately see the group of commandos bent on invading her workplace.

"You're quite a bit earlier than expect—" The words died in her throat as she looked up.

Before she could even reach for the radio at her hip, Summers was across the room. He pinned her arms behind her back with one hand and clamped the other over her mouth. Foster divested her of her keys and tossed them to Constantine before helping to secure her in the back of the truck. When a muffled whimper reached my ears at the same time as the coppery scent of blood flooded my nostrils, I realized they were taking the opportunity to feed.

Solana's body went rigid. Her eyes were suddenly dark, fathomless pools of thirst.

"Go," I said. "You need it. And you can make sure they don't kill her."

Faster than even I could perceive, she was gone. I joined Constantine, who was standing in front of the door flipping through the guard's key ring.

"Anything useful?"

He held one key aloft. "This one will get us inside. And this one might be for an elevator. We'll have to see."

As he perused the others, I let my gaze sweep over the nearly empty garage. "Why haven't we encountered any resistance?"

Constantine only shrugged. "Could be that Brenner is trying to lull us into a false sense of security. He rarely behaves in ways you'd expect. That's how he keeps his enemies off-balance."

I turned at the sound of footsteps to see Solana, Summers, and Foster approaching. The driver would stay with the truck to guard our escape route.

"Let's get in there."

Foster's words were clipped, her movements restless. Her blood high was in full swing, driving her to action. Constantine unlocked the door and she slipped inside behind him, but when I moved forward to follow, Summers held me back.

"Let them scout ahead."

Neither my panther nor I liked that idea, and we listened intently for any sound that might indicate a struggle. By the time they returned several minutes later, I was trembling with the need to hunt.

"There's a janitor working near the northwest corner of this floor," Constantine said. "Otherwise, it's clear."

"We're two levels below the lobby," added Foster.

Constantine dropped one of the keys into Summers's palm. "I couldn't test it without detection, but I'm reasonably sure that this one will call the elevator that opens directly into the Ty Warner suite."

"To be used only if feeling suicidal." Summers snorted in derision but pocketed the key. "Any last questions?"

I looked at my watch. The sun would rise in just over an hour. By now, Val should be in position. Her absence suddenly tore at me, and I stepped over the threshold hoping to find a measure of peace in forward motion.

The two groups split immediately, Foster and Summers heading toward the bank of elevators, and Solana, Constantine, and I ducking into the stairwell. The door creaked as I opened it, and I listened intently for the sounds of any movement above. When silence reigned, I edged up the first flight of stairs on my toes. As far as I could see, the landing above was empty.

But as we rounded the banister, I caught sight of a camouflaged figure on the stairs above, his semiautomatic pointed directly at my head. I spun away even as the silenced report of his gun quietly echoed between the walls, and I gritted my teeth in advance of the impact.

The bullet ripped into my shoulder, shredding muscle and shattering bone, and I embraced the pain as it set my panther free.

CHAPTER THREE

The acrid scent of gunpowder stung my nostrils as I leapt for my attacker. I felt the passage of his second bullet high above my head and saw the surprise in his eyes as I lunged for his jugular. My shift had taken mere seconds, and he hadn't been expecting that. His blood was hot in my throat and I tore at him greedily, desperate to assuage the hunger twisting my gut into knots. But even as I feasted upon my kill, I kept one ear cocked for sounds from above.

"Keep moving," I heard Constantine say as he and Solana edged up the next flight of stairs. "Don't let them reinforce their positions."

At the sound of a loud thud and muffled grunt, I raced to join them. Constantine was sprawled on the second floor landing, blood rushing from a nasty gouge in his forehead. Solana was grappling with a large man, her forearm pressed hard against his windpipe. As I watched, she kneed him in the groin. He doubled over, and I leapt to assist her, raking my claws along his back. The scream died in his throat when Solana slashed the butt of her gun across his temple. I turned back to Constantine in just enough time to see him convulse once before the space around his body blurred with the heat of his transformation. He emerged snarling, eyes fixated on Brenner's unconscious soldier.

While he fed, we continued our ascent. When the sound of growling erupted above us, Solana slowed her pace and hefted her weapon.

"They're prepared this time. I'll cover you when we get closer."

I growled in acknowledgment, tail lashing. Together, we crept up the next flight. I pushed my senses to their limit, straining for a sound or scent of the enemy above us. Constantine joined us at the halfway point, and I felt comforted by the press of his shoulder against mine.

With the advantage of stillness, they heard us first. The air erupted with the pings of silenced gunfire and Solana jerked away from the salvo. She crouched below the banister, expression grim.

Constantine butted his head against my flank and I turned to follow him. As we slunk along the wall, I braced myself for the chaos to come. We were trusting Solana to be able to cover us well enough to preoccupy any human gunman while he and I took on the four-footed soldiers. We padded gingerly along the landing, and suddenly, I caught the musky scent of wolf.

I didn't hesitate. Surging forward, claws extended, I darted around the corner. I tore through muscles and sinew but didn't take the chance to dig in and keep hold of my prey. Instead, I spun toward Constantine, racing back around the corner before the gunman's bullets could find me.

Taking advantage of his distraction, Solana darted into the open and returned fire. When Constantine and I crept out of concealment, the man lay sprawled along the top stair, blood pouring from a hole in the center of his forehead. The wolf was also bleeding from a gash in his right shoulder, but as Solana took aim, he fled. My paws skittered on the concrete as I sought to overtake him. For a moment, I felt like one of the figures in an Escher painting, but then the wolf's hindquarters came into view and I let instinct take over.

As one, Constantine and I leapt for him. I buried my teeth in the ruff of his neck as Constantine attacked his underbelly. Within moments, he was still. We stood panting over his body as Solana ejected the empty clip from her side arm and reloaded. She glanced at her watch.

"At this pace, we won't arrive in time."

I heard what she didn't say: that we needed to take more risks. I pressed forward more quickly than we had been, and Constantine and I took turns darting around the corners of each landing, trying to spring whatever traps they had laid for us. For several flights, we met no resistance. We had just passed the fourteenth story when suddenly, two wolves bounded onto the landing above, blocking both the stairwell and the door to the fifteenth floor. They paused for only an instant before racing toward us. I froze, but Constantine snarled and rushed to meet them. As he moved, a human figure hurtled into the space they had occupied, a pistol clutched in each hand. Time slowed as he pointed them both at my head.

If I ran toward him, would I be fast enough to evade his shot? Would Solana arrive in time to cover me? Even as the thoughts swarmed my brain, I was in motion. I bared my teeth as he drew down, gun barrel tracking my progress…and then the door crashed open to reveal Devon Foster, who didn't so much as hesitate before dispatching him. As Summers crowded in behind her, I shifted my trajectory to help Constantine with the wolves.

They had him cornered, and one had already scored a hit on his left flank. I darted in low, snapping at the legs of the nearest wolf who broke off his attack to face me. When I pounced, he backpedaled and managed to close his jaws on my right ear. Pain arced through me, bright and sharp, but when I kicked out in retaliation my claws hit home. Despite his grip on me, I twisted in his direction, forcing him to release me. Blood streamed into my eyes, but I followed his scent forward, lashing out with claws and teeth. When he faltered before the ferocity of my onslaught, I hung on to every part of him I could reach, snapping and battering blindly until he went still.

"Alexa. Alexa!"

Solana's voice pulled me out of my animal brain, and I sank back onto my haunches, blinking through the streams of red clouding my vision. Gentle hands stroked my neck as I panted against the pain.

Foster knelt before me. "Don't shift. You need your energy, and we can stop the bleeding if I tie a tourniquet."

I dipped my head in assent, and from behind me came the sound of fabric ripping. Solana entered my field of view and held out a piece of black cloth to Foster, who leaned forward to secure it to my ear. My nerve endings screamed, and it took an effort not to shy away. When Solana cupped my face with one hand and began to clean the blood out of my eyes, I focused on her gentle touch.

"Hurry," said Summers. "They're coming."

Brenner's soldiers were no longer making an effort to conceal their movements. The clattering of footsteps above was intermittently punctuated by the snarls of those in beast form. As Foster and Solana moved away, I looked to Constantine, who was licking his wound. Thankfully, it seemed shallow.

Summers gestured for us to stay pressed against the banister. As the approaching footsteps grew louder, he held up his hand and counted down on his fingers. When only his closed fist remained, he, Solana, and Foster leaned just far enough into open space to issue a salvo of bullets.

"Fuck!" Summers's gun clattered to the floor and a patch of red blossomed on his right forearm. "Just a nick," he hissed, eyeing his gun, which was now lying in the center of the landing. "But damn, that stings."

"We're outnumbered," said Foster.

"And out of time." Solana bit her lip, clearly fighting against despair.

"Well," said Summers, free hand clamped over his wound, "either we retreat or use the elevator."

Solana nodded. After a moment, so did Foster. I moved forward to brush against Solana's leg, indicating my agreement, and Constantine's answer had never been in doubt. If I died today, Val would be so angry at me for walking willingly into a trap. But this was now our only chance to beat Brenner at his own game, and if Val had been in my position, she wouldn't have turned tail, either.

"Make peace with your maker," Summers announced. He dropped a handful of shell casings over the railing, presumably in an effort to distract Brenner's soldiers. As they hit the floor, we made our dash for the door.

Their hail of bullets arrived just as we slid out of the line of fire. We raced down the empty hallway of the fifteenth floor, Foster leading the way toward the bank of elevators. Summers fumbled for the key, and as he fitted it in the lock to summon the elevator, we heard the sounds of pursuit. The elevator arrived as Brenner's troops pounded around the corner, and Foster and Solana laid down a fresh round of fire as the sliding doors closed. For several seconds, our harsh breaths were the only sound.

"This is suicide," Summers finally said, sounding oddly cheerful.

I knew he was right; everyone in the Ty Warner suite would see the elevator coming. They could beset us as soon as the doors opened, and we would be trapped.

I got as close as I could to the steel panel and prepared to leap for one of our assailants. Perhaps by surprising him, I could dodge a bullet. Constantine briefly touched his nose to my ear as he joined me at the door, and a purr rose in my throat at his gesture of affection.

The chime sounded. Valentine's face was before my mind's eye, handsome and loving and hungry. I would see her again. I had to believe it.

Slowly, the doors opened.

Chapter Four

As the suite's marble-tiled foyer came into view I pushed hard off the floor with my back legs, but my blind leap was not met by a snarling wolf or shower of bullets. The foyer was empty.

"What the fuck?" Summers stepped out of the elevator and surveyed the hall in disbelief.

An unearthly howl pierced the air and I felt my hackles rise. A burst of gunfire followed, but was cut off sharply by an agonized human scream. Solana raced past me toward the source of the sounds, and I followed at her heels. The corridor twisted once before opening onto a sitting room framed by a massive, floor-to-ceiling window.

Solana gasped and I crouched at her feet, every muscle tensed. The room looked like the set of a horror film. Swaths of fresh blood festooned the walls, the floor, and the opulent furniture. A large black wolf crouched over mangled human remains, gorging himself on his kill.

In the center of the room, a woman sat facing a brilliant sunrise. Her long, flaxen hair was resplendent in the golden glow, but her head was slumped forward and the sickly smell of burning flesh stung my nose. Her right hand was covered in blood, and more had dripped down to create a pool on the floor.

"Helen!" Solana was across the room before I could register her movement. Frantically, she dragged the chair into the hall, out of direct sunlight. As Foster and Summers rushed to help, Constantine and I positioned ourselves between them and the wolf.

"She's alive!" Foster announced triumphantly.

The human part of me rejoiced, but my animal brain was preoccupied by our canine adversary. He was behaving strangely. A low growl rumbled from his throat, but he had lowered his head and was backing away from his kill in a show of submission. Was he trying to indicate his surrender? Constantine at my side, I padded forward, alert to any sign that the wolf was bluffing.

We flanked him and began to herd him into a corner where his maneuverability would be compromised. After only a few steps, he stopped and held his ground. When I darted forward, snarling and snapping, he sank onto his belly, whining. As soon as I stood still, his body began to blur. My ears flicked backward at the sound of Summers's footsteps, and at the edge of my vision I caught the glint of daybreak off his gun barrel. Whoever this was, he was well and truly outnumbered.

My reaction to the tall man with shaggy dark hair who suddenly stood naked before us was wholly involuntary. I growled loud and long, ears flat against my head, tail lashing wildly. Sebastian Brenner had once dared to claim my mate as his own, going so far as to marry Valentine after she had lost her soul so they could both take advantage of the inheritance she had been able to collect upon wedding a man. For Val, their union had been only a business arrangement, but Sebastian had wanted to possess her fully, and for that, I could never forgive him.

"Sebastian Brenner?" Summers sounded even more surprised than I felt. "Explain yourself!"

Sebastian bared his teeth in an echo of his wolf's displeasure. Fists clenched at his sides, he took an assertive step forward, seemingly unfazed by his nudity in such a fraught situation.

"Back off, Leon. I came here to bargain for Helen's life."

"Bullshit."

Sebastian's face flushed. "If you won't trust me, then go ahead and shoot me. Wouldn't be the first time."

"Last I heard, you and Balthasar weren't on speaking terms. You expect me to believe you'd confront him on Helen's behalf?"

"My father takes great delight in begging. He would never listen to me, but I was hoping that if I kept him talking, I might learn something about his plans."

Summers finally lowered his side arm, but his finger remained a hairsbreadth from the trigger. "And did you?"

"He wasn't here."

"What?" Summers sounded as incredulous as I felt. "What do you mean he wasn't here?"

"There was no sign of him at all. I was trying to make a deal with one of his lieutenants, when someone fucking *shot* me." He palpated his left biceps, grimacing. "I shifted. The guards were too slow. Now they're dead."

When I realized that Val must have sniped Sebastian, the very human urge to laugh came on so strongly that I let it carry me into my transformation. Unashamed of my own nakedness, I raised my arms above my head, stretching my human muscles. Sebastian's face went blank as he looked me up and down, and I smiled in triumph. Mine was the body Valentine craved, the one she worshipped with her touch. Not his. Never his.

I turned to Summers. "We're safe. Let's contact Val."

As he hailed her over the com link, I went to the nearest closet. When I found several terrycloth robes hanging inside it, I tossed one to Sebastian before wrapping the other around myself. They probably cost hundreds of dollars, and I was happy to be charging them to Balthasar Brenner's tab.

The moment a fleeting smile crossed Summers's face, I let myself breathe again. Val was okay. We were going to make it through this.

"Yes, Alexa's fine," he said. "Helen is badly injured, but alive. What's your—"

"We need to get out of here," Foster called. The tension in her voice sliced through my relief. "Now. The police are on the way."

I turned to the sight of her gesturing sharply, her expression grim. Solana stood nearby, Helen in her arms. A damp towel covered

Helen's face and neck, and as I joined them I cringed at the charred scent that enveloped her. Helen's burns had to be very serious, and I wondered if she'd be able to make a full recovery.

I pressed close to Solana as we entered the elevator. She cradled Helen as gently as though she held an injured bird.

"How are you feeling?"

Her face was tearstained but resolute. "I'll feel much better when the physicians have examined her." She bared her teeth, and for a moment I was reminded of my first encounter with her in the jungle of Argentina. "He cut off her thumb! Why would he do such a thing?"

Unable to offer any answers, I rubbed her shoulder in comfort as the elevator descended. We were so close now, but as we exited into the garage, I heard sirens approaching. The truck rumbled into life and I jumped in after Summers, then turned to help Solana. Helen's head lolled against my shoulder as we raised her into the container, and when my stomach roiled, I focused on breathing through my mouth. She and I had never seen eye-to-eye, but all I could feel for her now was sympathy.

The truck lurched as the driver pulled out, and I crouched low to steady myself. Solana was whispering to Helen in Spanish, and I let the gentle cadence of her words soothe my own anxiety.

"Can you leave a different way than we entered?" Foster was asking the driver. "What kind of barricade? Just a chain? Smash through it, then. Hurry."

I braced myself between two wooden cartons, but the impact, when it came, was less than I'd expected. And then the truck began to tilt as the driver made a sharp turn much faster than he should have. For a moment, it felt as though we might jackknife, but with a bone-rattling thump, the truck finally settled back onto its axles.

"We have a problem," Summers said into the relieved silence. "I can't raise Headquarters."

"What?" Foster pulled out her phone, but Summers shook his head.

"Tried that already. Not the front desk, not the War Room, not the hospital wing. Nothing."

As I looked from face to face, I watched confusion give way to the realization that once again, Brenner had outmaneuvered us.

"We've been played." The epiphany sent chills shivering under my skin. "Helen's death sentence was a diversion. Brenner's been attacking Headquarters—"

"Probably since we left," Foster finished. "God damn it, we walked right into both traps."

"Are there countermeasures in place?" I asked, wondering what tools Karma had to work with as she tried to defend the people and resources threatened by Brenner. "What happens in the case of an invasion?"

"The War Room will be locked down," said Summers, "as will the hospital wing."

"How long will it take him to break into those areas?"

"Days." But Foster sounded uncertain.

"Hopefully, days," amended Summers. "Maybe hours."

"Helen certainly doesn't have days." The roughness of Solana's voice betrayed her inner turmoil. "She may not even have hours."

"We can go to the west-side hunting facility." Sebastian spoke for the first time since we'd descended from the penthouse. "It's a bare bones installation, but it does have a clinic."

"You don't think your father will deploy some of his troops there?"

"They're spread too thinly already."

I suspected he was right. Brenner had not only needed an attacking force, but also manpower to guard his vampire hostages, including Helen. He would likely focus on Headquarters and take the other Consortium outposts in the city later.

The truck began to slow. No sooner had it come to a halt than the container door was flung open. Valentine leapt inside, haloed by the rising sun. Her eyes found mine immediately, and within three long strides she had closed the distance between us. Our lips clashed in a kiss that was hot and fierce and far too brief.

All too soon, she pulled away and rested her forehead against mine. As I breathed in the cool, spicy scent of her, my world telescoped until it contained only us. We had endured this latest crucible unscathed. Others might call me naïve, but I truly believed that with Valentine at my side, all things were possible.

"We have to find a way to help Karma," I said, thinking of everything she had done for us, ever since I'd been a naïve but determined human.

Val cupped my face in her palms. "We will. We'll put our heads together and come up with a plan. But we need to regroup first."

"I know." My stomach chose that moment to rumble loudly. Shifting required an immense amount of energy, and I needed to eat as soon as possible. "I'm ravenous. Are you okay?"

"I'm fine. Only ran into a few security guards, and I was able to catch each of them by surprise."

The truck lurched back into motion, but Val's lightning reflexes kept us from stumbling. As we found a place to sit amongst the boxes, I saw her glance in Helen's direction. Solana was still bent over her, murmuring too quietly for me to hear over the throb of the semi's engine. I wondered what Val saw when she looked at them, and I got my answer when she grasped my hand a moment later.

"Thank you for never giving up on me," she said softly.

As I leaned my head against her shoulder, a wave of contentment washed over me. It should have felt incongruous in the midst of so much mayhem, but in that moment, all I could feel was gratitude.

CHAPTER FIVE

I toyed with my empty candy bar wrapper, daydreaming of the meal Val and I would share when this madness was behind us. I had a craving for steak—a rib eye cut, cooked black and blue, paired with a very expensive bottle of Shiraz. A long, leisurely dinner over which we would talk about nothing but our plans for the coming weekend or where we should travel on our next vacation or whether we should buy a second home out in the country.

Across the small, rickety table, Constantine balled up his empty bag of potato chips and tossed it into the garbage can next to the kitchen counter. He had shifted back into human form after hunting in the facility's subterranean arena. It was a far cry from the arena at Headquarters with its sun lamps and state-of-the-art climate control that could support both forested and prairie zones. This outpost on the west side served as a way station for Weres who found themselves in need. The kitchen shared the ground floor with a rudimentary infirmary and a small sitting room, and several floors of rooms above were available for anyone who needed a place to sleep for a night or two.

"What are you thinking?" Constantine asked.

"I'm imagining a real dinner."

His laughter reminded me of just how long it had been since I'd heard him express any measure of joy. For decades, Constantine had governed the secret Were city of Telassar, but Balthasar Brenner's army had forced him to abandon his post and go into hiding.

"That vending machine does leave much to be desired," he said.

The sound of Val's footsteps in the foyer brought a smile to my face. As she entered the kitchen I tilted my head back, inviting her touch. She began at my temples, massaging lightly in small circles, then continued down the nape of my neck with firmer strokes. Not wanting to make Constantine uncomfortable, I stifled the groan of pleasure that welled up from my chest.

"How is Helen?" Constantine asked.

Val stilled her hands. "Hard to tell. Solana's doing what she can."

I sat up with a sigh of regret. "Have Summers and Foster had any luck making contact with Headquarters?"

"They were still trying on the shortwave radio when last I saw them."

Constantine pushed his chair back and began to pace. "We need to make our move. Now. Every minute we wait gives Brenner more opportunity to secure his presence."

The sound of harsh whispers down the hall drew my attention to the threshold, where Summers and Foster appeared a few moments later. Their eyes were bloodshot, the skin around their lips taut with thirst and fatigue.

"We haven't been able to reach anyone," Summers said as he slid into the chair Constantine had vacated.

"That doesn't necessarily mean the worst, does it?" I asked. "They may be keeping quiet on purpose. Brenner might have the shortwave frequencies under surveillance."

"Perhaps." Foster leaned against the doorframe, fingers tapping restlessly against the chipped wooden surface. "As I see it, we have two options. The first is to wait for reinforcements and then mount some kind of offensive. The second is to go in now while Brenner is still preoccupied with taking full control of the building."

Constantine slapped both palms on the table. "Now."

Val laced her fingers with mine, and when I squeezed hard, she nodded. "We're in."

"There's a secret entrance we can try," said Summers. "A tunnel from the basement of the public library two blocks away. But the library has a metal detector, so we'll have to go in without guns."

"Where exactly does the tunnel lead?" I asked.

"The arena. Its opening is concealed in the forested section."

I reflected back to the last time I'd hunted there, only days ago. Even in my feline form, I hadn't sensed anything like what Summers was describing. That was encouraging. Besides, Brenner would most likely be focused on breaking into the War Room. With luck, the arena wouldn't yet be under surveillance.

Unexpectedly, I felt my panther stir. Disjoined images cascaded through my brain: a flash of tawny fur and red-gold mane; fierce, glittering eyes framing a broad muzzle; light glinting off wickedly curved teeth. They were the memories of my panther, forced across the thin barrier that separated her consciousness from mine.

"Malcolm! He might help us."

When everyone turned to look at me, I realized I'd spoken the thought. I couldn't think of him without also being reminded of Karma, and I tipped my head back to rest against Val's abdomen, trying to quiet the fluttering panic that filled my chest every time I imagined what Karma must be going through. Now was not the time for speculation. I had to believe she would be safe until we could come for her, but every intervening minute decreased the odds of her survival. Constantine was right. We didn't have the luxury of concocting an elaborate plan. We had to move.

"You might be right about Malcolm," Constantine acknowledged, and I felt my panther thrill to his words. Not only did she respect Malcolm's position as alpha Were, but she also wanted to see him avenged on Brenner. "But even if he doesn't come to our assistance, this plan has a fair shot at getting us inside undetected."

"We need to prioritize our objectives," said Val, "and I think the first order of business is to find any pockets of resistance so we can make a coordinated assault."

Summers shook his head. "That's a waste. We should focus on Brenner. Everyone in Headquarters will catch on once we're disrupting him."

"We can have it both ways," I said. "One group searches for allies while working on some kind of distraction. An explosion, maybe? Or triggering some kind of alarm? The other group takes a position near the center of action and waits to take advantage."

"Yes. Good." Constantine's eyes were bright. "The first group should be large, to firmly draw Brenner's attention to our target."

"But if the library has a metal detector, how will we smuggle in an explosive?" Summers's voice was tight with frustration.

"I have a small amount of C-4 on me," said Foster, unzipping one of the many pouches in her black vest and withdrawing a golf ball-sized lump that looked as though it were Play-Doh and not plastique. "If we hide the blasting cap on a key chain, we should make it through without any trouble."

"What if we target the hospital wing?" said Val. "Full of valuable equipment and medications." She leaned into me, her next words so soft the others didn't hear. "Besides, I hate that place. Dinging it up a bit will feel cathartic."

I stroked her face, anchoring myself against my own rush of memories featuring the Consortium's hospital wing: barging into the exam room where Val had first learned she was a vampire; falling into unconsciousness as my blood mingled with Sebastian's in a desperate attempt to synthesize a cure for Brenner's plague; imagining Valentine pale and inert, unable to protest as a stranger's blood dripped into her veins.

She was right. Setting off an explosion there would feel very good, indeed.

❖

The Kips Bay branch of the New York Public Library looked moderately crowded when Val and I entered an hour later. I fought my Midwestern impulse to smile at the man seated behind the circulation desk. If I did, I would stand out, and it was crucial that no one take special notice of me. As the "most innocuous looking" of the group, according to Summers, I had been chosen to carry the sphere of C-4. The detonator was tucked into a gaudy Statue of Liberty keychain I'd picked up at a nearby tourist shop.

We were the second pair to walk through the library doors, ten minutes behind Foster and Summers. We bypassed the elevator and turned into the stairwell. The first subterranean level was open to the public, but a chain link across the next flight proclaimed subsequent levels to be for employees only.

Val stepped over the chain and held out her hand. I laced our fingers together, not because I needed assistance, but because I needed so badly to feel her skin against mine. She had drunk from me again before we left Headquarters, and my body ached for fulfillment. The unabated hunger in her eyes was proof that she shared my need.

We had no time for indulgence, but I refused to leave our mutual desire unacknowledged. Now more than ever, we had to be open and honest with each other. When she would have continued on, I stopped her by threading my arms around her neck and pulling her head down for a long, slow kiss.

"I know what you crave," I murmured against her lips. "And I want your touch so badly. When this is over, we'll find the time. I promise."

Val's body shuddered. Sensing her frayed control, my panther paced restlessly behind my eyes—not out of fear, but anticipation. She too wanted what only Valentine could give us, and the craving put her on edge.

"We'd better keep moving." Val's voice was rough with arousal. "In another minute, I won't be responsible for my own actions."

I nipped at her chin as I reluctantly pulled away. Her sharp intake of breath would have made me smile on any other day. I took the lead as we continued along the stairs past a door leading to "Storage" and down another flight. The door to the lowest level was propped open, just as Summers and Foster had promised. As I ducked inside, I briefly wondered who had disabled the alarm.

My eyes adjusted almost instantly. A large boiler took up half the room, its internal machinery clanking.

"Here." Foster's call would have been inaudible to human ears. We joined them in a small alcove directly opposite the door, where they had already moved a set of shelves blocking the far wall.

The outline of a small door was visible through a layer of dust and cobwebs.

Summers fit a small key into the rusty lock. He had to jimmy it a few times before the bolt slid back, and at first, the door wouldn't budge. Val and I jumped in to set our shoulders to the warped wood, and at our second push, it swung inward. I was about to step into the passageway when I caught the familiar cadence of Constantine's footsteps from behind us as he brought up the rear of our group.

"Good timing," said Foster. "Let's get in there and cover our tracks."

The corridor ahead was pitch-black, and I gratefully accepted the headlamp Summers produced from his backpack. In feline form I could have relied on scent and touch to guide my way, but I didn't want to shift until it was absolutely necessary. Before locking the door, we laboriously moved the shelf back to its original position. Foster took point and I followed her, Val trailing behind me.

Aside from cobwebs and the occasional rat sighting, the tunnel was clear. Its gradual downward slope finally culminated in a rough stone wall, to which had been fixed a ladder leading to a circular trap door. Once everyone had gathered at the base of the ladder, Val took it upon herself to climb up. She stood poised at the top, one arm partially extended.

"Ready?"

I settled my pack more firmly on my shoulders and grasped the ladder rungs with both hands, wanting to be directly behind her when she emerged into the arena. As she pushed, the metal groaned and shivered. When she brought her other arm into play, the door finally popped open, hinges creaking. A shower of dirt rained down on us, and I shielded my eyes while holding my breath. Val was coughing so hard I feared she might fall, but when I risked a glance upward, her feet were just disappearing over the edge.

"No guards up top," she choked out.

Normally, several vampires were stationed along the catwalk just beneath the roof of the arena, their guns loaded with tranquilizer darts in case one Were decided to attack another. With Headquarters under siege their absence was unsurprising, but the fact that Brenner hadn't replaced them with his own soldiers was an encouraging sign. Our plan just might work.

Suddenly, the echoes of a menacing growl filtered down into the tunnel. Whether the beast was one of our own or one of Brenner's, it was likely to see Valentine as its next meal. Mustering every ounce of speed, I scrambled up the ladder and boosted myself over the edge. Several feet away, Val was crouched low, staring down the largest lion I'd ever seen. His red-gold mane framed a snarling face and his tawny body was on the verge of a pounce.

"Malcolm!"

The massive head turned in my direction, but he showed no sign of recognition.

"What's the plan here?" Val spoke softly and slowly, and I recognized her tone as one she had used with me often during my early days as a shifter. But Malcolm wasn't behaving like a Were; he was behaving like a beast. We needed reinforcements.

"Stay put," I told her, watching Malcolm shift his attention between us. "Send Constantine," I called into the tunnel.

Malcolm's lashing tail snapped the air and I knew we were out of time. Shrugging off my backpack, I dropped to my knees and uttered the word that would call my panther forth.

"Uje!"

CHAPTER SIX

As my paws hit the packed earth, Malcolm leapt for Valentine. In that moment, I didn't care who he was. My mate was in danger, and I would do everything in my power to keep her from harm. Newly formed muscles screamed in protest as I rushed for him.

His claws gleamed like knives as they sliced through the air, and I ducked beneath his reach, scoring a shallow hit across his broad chest. Roaring in pain, he crumpled prematurely to the ground and scrabbled for purchase along the forest floor. I positioned myself between him and Valentine, teeth bared.

I caught Constantine's scent, and in an instant he was standing beside me, fully shifted. As Malcolm got to his feet, Constantine gave voice to a long, menacing growl. For one fraught moment, it seemed as though Malcolm might charge, but then he sank onto his belly in a clear show of submission. He looked between us, seeming almost confused. Did he simply realize he was outnumbered? Or did he recognize us in our feline forms?

When I took a step forward, Valentine spoke my name. I twisted my head around to meet her eyes, hoping to reassure her. There was only one way to test whether Malcolm was dissembling. I approached him cautiously, a low purr rumbling in my throat. Once I was within his striking distance, I lowered myself to the ground and waited.

As his deep, chocolate eyes stared into mine, I willed him to remember—not only me, but himself. When he surged to his feet,

Val's sharp intake of breath pierced in my ears, but I held my ground. Regally, Malcolm bent his head and touched his nose to mine.

"Come on up," I heard Val call to Summers and Foster as Constantine took my place. "It's safe now. I think."

As the vampires appeared, a low growl rumbled up from Malcolm's throat, and he took several steps back, clearly uneasy in their presence. When Foster and Summers glanced warily at each other, then back at the tunnel, I was struck by the clear disparity between their abilities and mine. Having fed before we left, they had preternatural strength and speed on their side and could easily overpower a shifter in human form. But without a weapon, their only recourse against a beast of Malcolm's size and power was to run. Balthasar Brenner had founded his political philosophy on that discrepancy, and while myopic, his theories were all the more potent for containing a kernel of truth.

Constantine made a show of rubbing his shoulder against the vampires' legs and the clear display of trust seemed to settle Malcolm. Once Foster had replaced the trap door and covered it with a layer of dirt, we moved together toward the arena's entrance. Malcolm still seemed content to follow Constantine's lead, but I watched him closely. In his present state, he had the potential to be more of a loose cannon than an ally. We saw no sign of other Weres in the arena, but that was hardly surprising. Anyone who had been hunting when Brenner had invaded must have been alerted and called back into human form.

"Remember," said Summers as we reached the atrium and prepared to split up. "Don't initiate communication unless it's an emergency. Your explosion will be our sign to make a move."

He and Foster headed toward the nearest stairwell while we took the corridor that led around and behind the arena. The back staircase was closer to the hospital wing, and I was hoping it wouldn't be heavily guarded. We found no resistance at ground level, but Brenner's troops could easily have laid a trap for us behind the closed door.

Valentine crept forward on the balls of her feet, her movement soundless even to my ears. I padded beside her, but in a place frequented by a diverse mix of humans, animals, and vampires, even my keen senses were useless. When we arrived at the door, Val reached down to curl the fingers of one hand into the fur covering my neck. I glanced up at her and she nodded. We were going in blind with no weapons but her reflexes and my natural defenses, but at least we were going in together.

She released her grip and counted down from five. As her fist clenched, she flung open the door with her free hand and I raced inside, determined to surprise whoever lurked behind it.

But there was no one. At once surprised and relieved, I let my momentum carry me up the first flight of stairs, experiencing déjà vu as I once again crept cautiously around each blind corner. As the moments passed without any sign of our adversaries, I set a faster pace. The terrible hunger that always accompanied my transformation was growing stronger by the second. Already, I could feel my panther's instincts beginning to eclipse my human consciousness.

I stopped on the third-floor landing and sank into a crouch. Malcolm and Constantine took up flanking positions behind me, and Val trailed her fingers along my back as she crept silently toward the door. Again, she counted down. Again, I leapt for the open space as soon as she created it.

This time, they were waiting.

Two of Brenner's soldiers flanked the door, and as I barreled past them I saw them raise their guns in eerie synchronicity. I twisted in midair, ears flat against my head, willing my body out of their bullets' trajectory. One passed millimeters above my head. The other clipped my shoulder, and I snarled at the bolt of pain that flamed down my leg. I crashed to the floor, paws skidding along the tile. My injured muscles screamed in protest, but I forced my body forward, desperate to feel my enemies' flesh between my teeth.

Before I could reach them—before they could fire again—Constantine and Malcolm took advantage of the distraction I'd created. One gunman went down without noise. The other's hoarse shout became a wet gurgle that trickled off into silence. Valentine stepped out into the corridor and scanned in both directions before dropping into a crouch next to the bodies. Once she had deprived them of their weapons, she turned to face me.

"Are you all right, baby?"

I limped toward her, lines of fire radiating down my leg with each step. Val ripped an unbloodied patch of cloth from the shirt of one of Brenner's soldiers, then knelt to press it against my wound. When I gently butted her knee with my head, she stroked my uninjured side. I leaned into her touch until the sound of Constantine tearing into his kill reminded me of my hunger.

Belly twisting with the spasms, I edged closer to the two bodies. Constantine raised his head just long enough to growl, but Malcolm backed away from his kill. Last week in the arena I had shared prey with him, and now he was returning the favor. I wanted to believe this was another good sign—an indication that he was not totally lost to us.

As I approached the corpse, my hunger ascended, clawing its way up to supplant human reason. A film of red slid over my vision and I surrendered to my feline instincts, cleaving flesh from bone, knowing Valentine would protect me as I fed.

Finally, the urgency ebbed. As my human consciousness returned, I looked to Val who was inspecting her new weapons. Not so very long ago, I would have been ashamed to have her see me in a feeding frenzy. But we knew every aspect of each other fully now— the tender and the violent, the cutthroat and the compassionate, the dark and the light. She was my mate. I felt her in my soul and claimed a place in her body's every cell.

"If those guards weren't alone, we'll have company," she said, her voice barely above a whisper. "Alexa, are you okay to go on?"

My right leg was stiff and sore, but the flow of blood had stopped and I dipped my head in assent. If I shifted back and forth again, I would be healed but dangerously weak. It was better to carry on, but I let Malcolm and Constantine share the lead as we moved forward.

Ahead, the corridor ended in a T. The silence was oppressive. Every other time I'd visited this floor, the distant beeping of heart monitors and the hustle and bustle of human orderlies had filled the air. Were there no patients in the infirmary, or had they been evacuated? Or worse…

Suddenly, the walls themselves seemed to sigh in a low hissing noise that came from somewhere to our left. I froze, every sense extended. The sound didn't repeat itself, but I knew I hadn't imagined it. Constantine and Malcolm quivered beside me, hackles raised. If Val's reflexes hadn't been so sharp, she would have crashed into them. The question in her eyes was obvious, but she didn't speak and her finger hovered just above the trigger of her firearm.

I began to move forward, but her hand on my flank made me pause. She shook her head once before flattening herself against the wall at the edge of the intersection. I let her go. Now that she was armed, she could lay down cover fire for us if necessary.

In one fluid movement, she spun into the open, gripping her weapon with both hands. When her shoulders dropped infinitesimally, I knew we were clear to join her. She set a quick pace down the hall, which ended in a sliding door. I had never been inside the laboratory, but if its door was pressurized, that could have been the source of the mysterious sound. Still, that meant someone had opened or closed it—someone who would doubtless be waiting for us. As we approached, Constantine and Malcolm fanned out to flank Valentine, leaving me to guard her back. Exactly where I wanted to be.

Without any warning, Val broke into a run. After a split second of confusion, we leapt into motion behind her. As she triggered the door, she dropped into a slide along the slick tiles. Gunfire erupted from the threshold, but the bullets passed above us. I heard the sharp report of her weapon and then the gunman slumped to the floor, a quarter-sized hole in the center of his forehead.

Valentine never stopped moving, instead using her momentum to propel herself back onto her feet. But just as she regained her balance, another human figure stepped out of concealment behind the door. He was too close to fire, but he swung viciously at her head with the butt of his assault rifle. Faster than I could follow, Val dodged the blow just far enough so that it caught her in the shoulder. The coppery scent of her blood filled the air as she staggered and crashed into the wall.

Rage welled up in me, eclipsing the pain of my injury. But even as I raced to Val's defense, two wolves emerged from the shadows behind the door. Constantine and Malcolm rushed forward to meet them, and the air filled with the sounds of snapping and snarling. For a moment, it seemed as though Val's assailant would land another strike with his weapon, but she ducked his next blow and delivered a powerful uppercut that snapped his head back. By the time I'd arrived at her feet, she had lunged to the side, raised her gun, and dispatched him.

Despite the blood streaming down her arm, Val didn't so much as pause to catch her breath. Swiftly, she swung the bag down from her shoulders and began to set the explosive charge. As she worked, I rejoined Malcolm and Constantine, who were licking minor wounds after their most recent fight.

And then, over the antiseptic flavor of the air and the pungent musk of Were sweat and the metallic odor of blood, I caught his scent. Balthasar Brenner. I would have recognized it anywhere, and though my human brain flooded over with remembered fear and anxiety, my animal instincts knew only rage.

When his scent grew stronger, I realized he was approaching from the corridor intersecting this hallway just a few feet ahead of us. Val was oblivious, and I had no time to make her understand. I charged into her, throwing her off-balance and sending her skidding toward the right-hand alcove just inside the door. She grunted in pain, but I turned away, paws scrabbling at the tile as I tried to build up momentum. Before I could gain purchase on the floor, Malcolm shot past me. He reached the corner just as Brenner stepped around it. The world slowed as Malcolm bowled into his nemesis, claws extended. Gunfire echoed between the walls and blood spattered across the gleaming floor, a crimson Rorschach blot.

A hush fell over the corridor. Malcolm's back legs twitched, but otherwise, there was no sign of movement. I edged closer, my senses straining. Had Malcolm triumphed, only to be struck down himself? Was Brenner still alive?

Suddenly, Malcolm flopped onto his side. I had only a second to realize my mistake before I flattened myself into the alcove across from Valentine, barely evading the barrage of bullets that sprayed into the hall. Brenner was manipulating Malcolm's injured body—using him as a shield. There was nothing I could do to get to him, short of putting myself in the line of fire. Val caught my eye and shook her head, then hefted her rifle. I understood; she would try to keep Brenner distracted. Perhaps she would even get lucky.

But as she began to return fire, it quickly became clear that Brenner had the superior tactical position. Val had to take care with her shots so as not to further injure Malcolm, whose back legs continued to scrape weakly against the floor. He seemed to have lost all control of his front legs, and Brenner could easily have put him out of his misery. Doubtless, he realized we'd be less aggressive if he allowed Malcolm to live.

Each time I tried to take advantage of Val's cover fire, Brenner managed to force me back into the shadows. When I turned to catch a glimpse of Constantine, I found him trapped just outside the lab. His weight held the door open, but whenever he tried to make his way toward me, Brenner sprayed the corridor with bullets.

At first, I thought the roaring in my ears was the sound of my own frustrated growls. But then the rumble grew louder, punctuated by a rhythmic throbbing more felt than heard. When the very walls began to pulse, I finally recognized the source. Rotor blades. Someone was flying a helicopter very close to this building.

Suddenly, Brenner was racing down the corridor away from us, toward the window at its far end. He kept his rifle pointed backward, providing his own cover as he ran. Val's curses echoed in my ears as I waited for him to lower his weapon. Just a few seconds—I could reach him in just a few seconds. Muscles taut, I waited for my opening.

It came moments later, when he swung his rifle across the front of his body, finger still pressed to the trigger. The window exploded outward, glass splinters gleaming prismatically in the influx of sunlight. I bounded toward him, leaping over Malcolm, milking every ounce of energy from my wounded body. Valentine's bullets whistled above me, and I saw Brenner jerk as one of them struck him below his left shoulder blade.

Too little, too late. He leapt for the window, body corkscrewing into open space as his momentum punched him through the remaining glass shards. The dark and tangy scent of his blood bloomed on the air, and screams from passersby below rose up to us like a descant. I skidded to a halt at the far wall and braced my paws on the sill, craning my neck for a glimpse.

Had I been human, I would have gasped. Brenner clung to one of the helicopter's landing skids, tilting it precariously as it struggled to clear the roof of the high-rise across the street. In the next second, Val was beside me. She raised her gun and sighted along the barrel, jaw clenched in concentration. Helpless, I prayed she would find her mark…but as she squeezed the trigger, the chopper accelerated sharply upward. Val's shot hit the skid just past Brenner's grip, inciting more screams from the spectators below.

"Fuck!" Val hurled her weapon to the floor as she watched Brenner escape into the darkening sky.

I let my panther's bewildered rage incite my transformation. As the bone-jarring pain of my shift subsided, I released a long breath and returned my attention to Val, who was speaking tersely into her phone.

"You heard me—gone. Call in all the favors you have left to hold off the police. We're going to try to figure out what Brenner was looking for here in the first place."

"Foster?" I asked when Val vehemently disconnected the call.

She nodded, then reached out a hand to me. Her fingers were trembling with suppressed rage, but her touch on my face was exquisitely gentle. "How are you feeling?"

I managed a thin smile. "Good as new. Though I could eat a horse."

"Alexa!"

At Constantine's strangled shout, I spun to face him. He was standing over Malcolm, and at first, I feared the worst. But then I registered the haze surrounding him as his massive body began to blur. After weeks spent trapped in his lion, Malcolm was finally shifting back into human form.

We had lost Brenner, but regained our general.

CHAPTER SEVEN

Where the massive lion had lain half-paralyzed, a broad-shouldered man now knelt taking deep, shuddering breaths. Malcolm's golden brown hair, shot through with white at his temples, was matted with sweat. He stared straight ahead as though blind, unable or unwilling to respond to his surroundings. When Constantine crouched and tentatively touched his shoulder, a shiver wracked his frame.

"Malcolm?"

He blinked, then sat back on his heels as his dark, solemn eyes flared with recognition. "Constantine."

"That's right." Constantine's voice was thick with joy and relief. "You've returned to us."

"Welcome back," I said, leaning into Val as she rested one hand between my shoulder blades.

"Alexa." When his gaze settled on Valentine, he frowned in confusion. And no wonder—the last time Malcolm had seen me, just before he was shot, Val had been my nemesis and not my lover.

"I'll find something for you all to wear," she whispered before ducking into the corridor.

Malcolm watched her walk away, then looked around the hallway, clearly confused. "Balthasar. Was he here, or did I imagine it?"

"He was here." Constantine's jaw clenched around the syllables.

"You fought him," I said. "But he escaped."

Malcolm snarled beneath his breath, and despite my exhaustion, my panther leapt to his call. I held her back, soothing her, reminding her that right now there was nothing we could do. We needed to bide our time and rest for the next hunt.

"What else do you remember?" said Constantine.

Malcolm stood, a little unsteadily, and walked to the broken window. "I can recall meeting at your home to discuss Balthasar's recent movements," he said. "Everything afterward is fragmented—like a dream."

His anxiety was plain. "And that's not normal for you?" I asked. "Not usually the way you perceive your lion's memories?"

"No."

Constantine and I exchanged a glance, and after a moment, I nodded. Malcolm was looking stronger by the second, and he needed to know what had happened to him.

"You were shot in the head outside my brownstone," Constantine said.

Malcolm didn't turn around. "How long ago?"

"Just over a month," I said. "You were in a coma for a week, and then you shifted. But you showed no sign of returning to human form until…now."

At that moment, Val returning holding a pile of light blue clothing in her arms. "I found some scrubs."

I sifted through the pile until I found a pair that looked to be the right size. As I pulled them on, Val's phone rang again. She answered, then mouthed "Foster" to us.

"Before you finalize any plans," she said after a few moments, "you should know that Malcolm has made a full recovery. He's with us in human form. He might know something about Brenner's motives."

Within seconds, she was returning the phone to her pocket. "Summers and Foster will be back in touch as soon as they've made sure the rest of the building is secure." She looked to Malcolm, who was just pulling on one of the scrub shirts. "Do you have any idea why Brenner would come straight to this lab instead of attempting to take over the War Room, as we expected?"

"Our medical and experimental data is housed in this wing," said Malcolm. "But the records room is inaccessible to everyone except Helen and myself."

I looked from Val to Constantine, dread spiraling in my stomach. "Does the security mechanism use biometrics?"

Malcolm nodded. "A DNA match to open the door, and a thumb scan to access the computer console inside."

Constantine cursed under his breath. "Brenner got to Helen. We can assume he was able to pull whatever data he wanted."

"He got to Helen?" Alarm was written plainly on Malcolm's face. "Is she still alive?"

"She is, but badly wounded," said Val. "As of this morning, she hadn't regained consciousness."

"Can you find out what he accessed?" I asked. "We might be able to predict his next steps."

"Yes." Malcolm gestured for us to follow as he moved down the side corridor. Val slipped her hand into mine as we trailed him.

"How are you holding up? You must be exhausted. And starving."

"I'll be okay for a little while longer." I trailed the fingers of my free hand along her left forearm. "You're the injured one. How's your shoulder?"

"Getting stiff."

Even that much of a confession was a clear indication that she was feeling more pain than she let on. "You need to feed, sweetheart."

"Not until you've eaten."

I would have protested, but Malcolm halted in front of a door on the left side of the hallway. He pressed one fingertip to a small black panel on the wall and I caught the faintest scent of blood. The DNA test.

A moment later, the door slid open to reveal a large rectangular room resembling a bank's safe deposit vault. Hundreds of small compartments had been built into the walls. Each bore an alphanumeric string in bold black letters, but none had any kind of physical locking mechanism. In the center of the room, a computer console rested on an otherwise empty desk.

"The only way to access the data vault is to log into the computer," Malcolm explained as he sat in the high-backed leather chair in front of the screen. When he slid his right thumb across a metallic strip on the keyboard, I couldn't help but envision how Brenner had tricked the computer. For the first time in my life, I winced in sympathy for Helen.

The screen lit up and Malcolm input a username and password. Once into the system, he typed a series of command-line prompts that immediately generated a long stream of data. As he scanned the information, his fingers once more flew over the keys.

"According to the computer, the last person who logged in was Helen, barely half an hour ago."

"That was Brenner," I said grimly. "What did he access?"

After pressing a few more keys, Malcolm sat back in the chair, one knuckle pressed to his chin. "A box containing data from some of our research into the vampire parasite."

"What?" Val went rigid against me.

"I'm not familiar with the project," said Malcolm. "But this file lists the contents of the box as a flash drive and several frozen samples. We can see if he removed anything."

Seconds later, one of the panels near the bottom left corner of the room hissed open. We crowded around the empty, stainless steel tube.

"Whatever it was," said Constantine, "he took it all."

"Helen will have more details. The project title is in the records." Malcolm didn't sound pleased with his ignorance.

Val fished her phone from a pocket. "I'll call Solana to see whether Helen's in any shape to speak with us."

Malcolm's gaze followed Valentine as she exited into the hallway, where she could get a clearer signal. He faced me as soon as she was gone.

"Valentine is no longer a full vampire. How?"

"It's a long story," I said, "but thanks to Karma's research, I was able to track down a rare herb with the ability to bring her back."

"Permanently?"

I looked over my shoulder to where Val paced before the door as she spoke into the phone. "We don't know for sure yet. She needs to run some tests."

"Still. Impressive."

"Speaking of miraculous recoveries," Constantine said, "it may be wise for you to consult a physician as soon as possible."

Malcolm gave him a withering look, and I bit back a smile. Val returned before he could reply, and I could tell from her expression that Solana's news wasn't wholly positive.

"Helen is still unconscious. She is being transported here as we speak. Solana has promised to let us all know the moment she wakes."

"Who is Solana?" Malcolm was sounding more on edge by the minute, and I sympathized with his frustration. He had been thrust back into his human mind and body at the precise moment when the Consortium—his life's work—had reached a crisis point.

"A former lover of Helen's." Constantine's voice was carefully neutral. "From well over a century ago."

"With or without Helen, we will reconvene at midnight." Despite being out of touch, Malcolm was clearly back in charge. He looked to each of us in turn. "In the War Room. Meanwhile, you should all rest. God only knows when we'll next have an opportunity to catch our breath."

I wanted nothing more than a few precious hours alone with Val, but I also knew my place. "You're certain there's nothing I can do?"

Malcolm shook his head. "Go. I will have Karma bring me up to date."

When Val reached for my hand, I let her lead me toward the door. "I'm so thirsty for you," she whispered softly enough that only I could hear. "Let's not waste another second."

My hunger, my fatigue, my worry—they all melted away in the face of her need, and I followed her willingly.

❖

An hour later I sat back in my chair, surveying the remains of my steak. Valentine had cooked it perfectly, and I was relieved to no longer be consumed by the gnawing hunger that had preoccupied me since my return to human form. Across the table, Val regarded me with an expression half-loving, half-hungry. Her own meal was similarly demolished, but I knew what she truly craved.

She moved to lace her fingers behind her head but winced as the motion aggravated her injury. Her smile was rueful. "And how was your day, honey?"

Laughing, I covered one of her hands with my own. "Probably the craziest on record."

"There may be crazier on the horizon."

Beneath her flippancy lurked a current of…not fear, exactly, but perhaps anxiety. Brenner's theft implied that he was going to use the parasite for some nefarious purpose—a theory worrisome to all of us, but especially the vampires. Brenner's agenda was very simple: genocide. He wanted to eliminate the presence of vampires on the planet. The last time he had gotten his hands on a biological agent, he had turned it into a powerful weapon that would have killed me had Val not discovered the means to create a cure. This time, it seemed far more likely that she was the target.

Just as we had sat down to dinner, Val had received a text from Solana. Helen had regained consciousness, and while she was still very weak, she would be attending the meeting later tonight. Hopefully, she would have some answers that would set us on the right track.

"We'll find Brenner," I said, knowing Val would hear the sentiment beneath the platitude. "We'll stop him."

She flipped over her hand and slid her fingers against mine. The slow, brushing strokes of her skin set my own ablaze.

"I don't want to think about him right now," she said. "I just want to focus on you."

The intensity behind her words spiked my pulse. "I love the way you make me feel. Like there's no one else on the planet but us."

Val leaned forward, blue eyes blazing. "Tell me what you want, most of all in the world, right now. Anything. Whatever it is, it's yours."

Her offer was sincere. I could have asked for the thousand-dollar ice cream sundae at Serendipity, and she would have called the restaurant without a second thought. Other women might have used a moment such as this to ask for jewelry or a new pair of shoes, but all I wanted was the sensation of Valentine above me, beneath me, inside me.

First, though, I wanted to tease her. "Do you realize that I haven't yet experienced the hot tub?"

Val's burst of laughter did nothing to dissolve the glorious tension flowing between us. "That's easily fixed."

I stood and slowly removed my shirt. I wore nothing beneath it. "How about right now?"

Her breathing hitched and her eyes darkened. When I peeled off my jeans, she bared her teeth.

"Sure you don't just want to go to bed?" Her voice was a solid octave lower than normal.

"Not yet. I want to soak for a while." But when she moved to join me right away, I held up one hand. "Stay exactly where you are."

After so much chaos and death, having the time to indulge in a sensual interlude felt like a luxury. Desire suffused my blood and I throbbed with the urgency of it, but I didn't want to rush. Naked, I descended the half-flight of stairs to where the tub waited, already roiling merrily. My hips swayed as I walked, and above the churning of the water jets I heard Valentine sigh in appreciation.

When I reached the edge, I turned to face her, then lowered myself to the tile and immersed my feet. The water was very hot and I eased myself into it by inches, watching Val's hungry gaze roam across my misted skin.

"You're killing me." The softly groaned words would have been inaudible to a human.

"I'm not. I'm going to heal you." With a slow exhale, I slid all the way into the tub until only my head remained above the water line. "Now, come here."

She vaulted down the stairs and was at my side in the space of a blink. Her chest rose and fell rapidly as she disrobed, and when she finally stood nude before me my mouth went dry. Valentine often passed for a man, but her naked body was the paragon of feminine strength. Her long, runner's legs gave way to a lightly rippled abdomen and full breasts, framed by chiseled arms strong enough to hold me tightly when I needed comfort and hold me down when I needed to be dominated. Right now, I wanted to bury my face in the flaxen hair between her thighs, and I gripped the edge of the tub to stop myself from moving. We were going to take this slowly, even if it killed us both.

Her sigh of pleasure at the water's heat became a hiss of pain when she submerged her injured arm. I pressed myself against her side and rubbed the back of her neck until she relaxed.

"I love your hands on me," she murmured.

In response, I kissed first her shoulder, then her neck. When I trailed my lips along her jaw line to flick my tongue against her earlobe, her self-restraint finally shattered. In an instant, she was looming above me, my legs trapped between her knees, her fingers curled in my hair.

"Enough!"

Despite the heat of the water, my skin pebbled at her assertive tone. When I tried to speak and failed, triumph flared across the stark planes of her face. The tide had turned, and I waited with open arms for it to engulf me.

"I need to be inside you," Val rasped. Darkness eclipsed her brilliant blue irises as her thirst magnified her desire. "Every way, all the way. No more waiting."

Finally, I found my voice. "I'm yours. Take me."

I expected her to strike quickly, anticipating a swift surge of pain followed by the slow bloom of ecstasy. Instead, she covered my neck and collarbone with searing kisses until I was begging for her teeth. Only then did she claim me fully, sliding her canines into my jugular.

She cradled my head as she drank, her gentle touch playing counterpoint to the necessary violence of our joining. I thrilled to the sensation of her lips hollowing around my skin; of my blood being drawn deeply into her body. My inner beast was alert and on-guard, but she recognized the touch of her mate. And when Valentine slowly began to ease her free hand along the taut muscles of my inner thigh, the panther's contentment radiated from the depths of my brain, as though she was purring.

"Yes," I gasped as Val drew closer to the center of my need. "Please touch me."

Her mouth at my neck became less insistent as she slipped inside. When she filled me up, I cried out her name. When she twisted her fingers, I screamed. When she finally tore her lips from my skin, I cupped the nape of her neck with one hand and pulled her in for a long, passionate kiss.

Her thumb moved over me, her fingers inside me, but I couldn't let go until I knew that she too was on the edge. With my free hand, I found her wet and swollen. As she moved in me I moved in her, and when she broke the kiss to breathe I held her close, our foreheads pressed together, each reading the signs of the other's approaching ecstasy.

"Mine," she gasped against my lips, her eyes losing their focus. She was very close, and I gloried in her lack of control.

"Yours. Always. I love you, Valentine."

At my words, her body clenched around me. The sound of my name on her lips propelled me over the precipice with her, and in my last lucid moment, I knew only peace.

CHAPTER EIGHT

I woke to the sound of an angry wasp nest. Alarmed, I sat up quickly, only to discover Valentine beside me fumbling with something on the nightstand.

Her buzzing phone, not stinging insects. Slowly, I reoriented to my surroundings. My feet were tangled in crimson sheets on a king-sized bed, and floor-to-ceiling windows revealed the glittering cityscape below. We were in our SoHo apartment, and it was almost ten o'clock in the evening. I'd been asleep for nearly three hours, but despite my body's accelerated regeneration, I was still exhausted. I let myself sink back down onto the blankets and curled around Val, who had pushed herself up into a sitting position.

I smoothed my palm down her thigh. "We can sleep for another hour, can't we?"

"I could sleep for another month." Her voice sounded as gritty as my eyes felt, but she leaned over to kiss my forehead before slipping from the bed. "That was the bank, not my alarm. I need to call in. Stay and rest, baby."

Naked, she padded toward the door. I watched her go, then pulled the covers up to my chin and allowed the distant cadence of her voice to lull me into a doze. As I hovered between sleep and waking, daydreams—both feline and human—flickered before my mind's eye. After so much chaos, the images were gloriously mundane: lounging in the shade of a lone tree on the savannah, sharing a meal with Val at an outdoor café, holding her hand as we walked along the Hudson in full daylight. I clung to the mental pictures, sifting through their layers, craving a time when we could bring them all to pass.

At the sounds of Val's return, I knew our momentary respite had come to an end. Her footsteps were quick and purposeful, and I opened my eyes in time to see her fling wide the doors of the walk-in closet.

"What happened?"

She turned just enough for me to observe her clenched jaw. "Christopher Blaine."

Fatigue forgotten, I slid to the edge of the bed. Presidential candidate Christopher Blaine had some kind of strong connection to Brenner, though no one in my circle knew the precise nature of their relationship. "What did he do?"

Wooden hangers clacked together loudly as she searched for something to wear. "He's coming after vampire assets, and my bank is directly in his crosshairs."

I stepped inside and began to dress. "At Brenner's orders, do you think?"

"Don't you?" When she noticed what I was doing, she stopped buttoning her shirt. "Baby. You should stay. Get a little more sleep, and I can meet you at Headquarters."

I took a step closer to her, running my palm across her taut abdominal muscles before doing up her remaining buttons. "No. I don't want to be parted from you."

That made her smile, and she lightly caressed my cheek before leaning in for a gentle kiss. "All right."

During the elevator ride, I toyed with her French cuffs, spinning the bull-shaped links back and forth. As the sign of both the Order of Mithras and a burgeoning economy, the bull was an especially appropriate symbol for her to wear. Dressed in a dark charcoal suit over a red-and-white striped shirt, Valentine cut an imposing figure. She exuded a blend of confidence and ambition as heady as an expensive cologne. As the daughter of the Secretary of the Treasury, Val had grown up surrounded by the world of high finance, and it showed. Banking might not have been her calling, but she was adept at playing the game.

"You know," I said, "I almost feel sorry for Blaine."

"Oh?"

"I know that you and your father don't exactly see eye to eye, but you've managed to combine his best qualities without expressing his worst ones."

"That's a relief." She linked one arm through mine as we emerged into the crisp night. "I don't want to do this forever, though. I still think about going back to medicine."

I half-turned toward the nearest subway station before remembering that our driver was waiting at the curb. It was going to take some time for me to become accustomed to the perks of our new existence.

"Don't forget," I said as she settled into the backseat next to me. "Forever is exactly what we have. Plenty of time to try all kinds of careers."

She walked her fingers along the seam of my slacks in a caress at once reassuring and arousing. "Once we've dealt with Brenner, let's take a century off to do nothing but sleep and make love."

"Oh, that sounds so good."

For the remainder of the ride, I leaned my head against her shoulder and emptied my mind of everything but the sensation of being close to her. Only when Val directed the driver to drop us off at the front entrance did I pull away to smooth out the minor wrinkles in my blouse and run a hand through my hair. Oddly, I felt self-conscious—perhaps because I held no official role at the bank and would be there only as Valentine's lover.

"You look fantastic," Val murmured as we entered the lobby.

She hadn't read my mind, but she had probably picked up on my body language. I squared my shoulders and reached down to lace our fingers together. Whatever my minor insecurities, I had to project an air of confidence. This was vampire territory, and the widespread renewal of hostility between our species meant that I had to tread carefully.

Val kept my hand firmly clasped in hers as we made our way across the crowded atrium. Heads turned and whispers followed in our wake. I wondered how much of the attention was due to the events that had just transpired at Headquarters, and how much simply had to do with Valentine's emergence as a major player in the vampire world at this particularly chaotic time. While we could have arrived via her private entrance, she needed to be visible right now. Her presence would improve chances for stability—not only for the Bank of Mithras, but also for the Consortium.

Three people were waiting in the anteroom of her office: Kyle Jordan, and a man and woman I didn't know. Kyle, whose puppyish enthusiasm had persisted even after Val had turned him into a vampire, looked excited to see me. The other man put me immediately on edge despite his wiry build and average height. He was dangerous. I knew it instinctively.

Like him, the woman betrayed no emotion as she stood to greet us. About my height, she had eyes and hair of the same rich chocolate shade. A surge of possessiveness made me dig my nails into Valentine's hand before I even knew what I was doing. Val stroked her thumb once over my knuckles in silent reassurance.

"Bridget and Caleb, this is my partner, Alexa Newland. Alexa, Bridget manages the new brokerage services wing of the company and Caleb is my head of security."

"Pleasure." My handshake was firmer than Bridget's, and she quickly disengaged. Caleb only offered a shallow nod.

As the door closed behind us, Val shrugged off her jacket. With it went the air of formality she had cultivated while we were under public scrutiny in the lobby. She gestured toward the conference table. "Let's sit. Caleb, I haven't yet checked in with Headquarters. Any news on Brenner's whereabouts?"

"A few leads, but nothing solid yet." He waved away the glass of scotch she tried to hand him. "I haven't put many of our people on the chase. Do you want that to change?"

"No. If Blaine is after us, we're going to need them here." Val sat in the chair at the head of the table. "Speaking of which: all I know is what Bridget told me on the phone—that Blaine is using his pull with the SEC to launch an investigation."

Bridget withdrew a pair of glasses from her small purse and opened the file folder she had carried in with her. "Not only the

SEC. He's also reached out to the rating agencies, and to a few watchdog groups."

Val leaned back in her chair. "What's the motive, here? Is he just trying to drum up negative publicity to make our investors lose confidence? Or is there more to it? Do we have any sense of his long-term goals?"

"I'm of the opinion that whatever Blaine is up to, it somehow fits into Brenner's plan," said Caleb. "On the one hand, he might simply be trying to create a panic. On the other hand, he may be after something bigger. I've put both our physical and cyber security teams on full alert."

Val drummed her fingertips on the tabletop. "I want to know his motives. Until we do, we'll only be able to react, and I don't like getting caught flat-footed."

"What about the legality of all this?" I asked, trying to remember back to the courses I'd taken that had included a corporate law component. "Does he have any kind of just cause for sending these agencies after us?"

"The Consortium's legal counsel has been informed," said Bridget, "but right now, as you can imagine, they're focused on other matters."

The possibility of putting some of my education to use while also protecting Val was highly attractive to me. Despite having taken a leave of absence from NYU Law, I still had plenty of contacts there whom I could call on.

"If I can help, I will."

"I know this cover-your-ass stuff is important," said Val, "but I'd rather kick his ass instead. Give him a taste of what he's dishing out. Can we brainstorm some ways to distract him and hit him where it hurts at the same time?"

As the others began to toss out suggestions, I surreptitiously ran my heel along Valentine's calf muscle. Going on offense against Blaine was a smart idea, and right then I decided I wouldn't wait for Bridget, or the beleaguered Consortium, to ask for my help. At the earliest possible moment, I would take matters into my own hands. It would take a lot of cramming on my part, but I would find a way to bring a suit against Blaine while Val's people worked to destabilize him in other ways.

After a few more minutes of discussion, she pushed her chair back from the table. "We need to get to Headquarters. Caleb, will you do some digging to see which of these angles seem most fruitful?"

"Of course."

"We'll reconvene soon. In the meantime, let's play stall ball every step of the way."

Val answered a few additional questions as she walked them out. After she closed the door behind them and turned around, she discovered that I'd taken the liberty of testing out the high-backed leather chair behind her desk.

Her eyes darkened perceptibly. "You look devastatingly attractive in my chair."

Instead of letting on how deeply her words affected me, I arched one eyebrow. "Oh?"

"Someday soon, I'm going to make love to you, right there, until you scream." She glanced at her watch again. "Unfortunately, it can't be today."

I went to her, threading my arms around her neck and pulling her down for a long, slow kiss. Her tongue slid possessively against mine, and for one sweet moment, I let myself forget all about the chaos around us.

"I'll be counting down the seconds," I whispered against her mouth.

❖

Headquarters swarmed with security officers, each of whom held an automatic rifle. They stood in pairs—one vampire, one wereshifter—and regarded each other just as suspiciously as they did those who entered the building. We had to show our identification four separate times before we were granted access to the conference room next to Helen's office.

We entered to find Malcolm, Karma, Solana, and Helen already present. Malcolm stood before the large bay windows that looked out over the dark swath of the East River and the colorful lights of Long Island City, speaking softly with Karma. Solana was perched on one arm of the leather sofa along the far side of the room next to Helen, who lay propped up on several pillows. Her face and arms were almost entirely covered with bandages, but her eyes were alert and focused as she watched us enter the room. Val led us to her, then dropped into a crouch so Helen wouldn't have to crane her neck.

"Helen. How are you feeling?"

"As well as can be expected," she rasped. She was trying hard not to open her mouth too widely, and as a result her words were slightly garbled.

Val looked from her to Solana. "Is there anything you need from me?"

"At the moment, no." Solana smiled ever so slightly when I reached across to squeeze her hand. "Thank you."

The door opened again to admit Constantine, followed by Summers and Foster. Constantine looked as though he wanted to join us, but then Malcolm turned and gestured toward the table. With the exception of Solana and Helen, we each found seats. Dark circles prevailed beneath bleary eyes for nearly everyone at the table. Malcolm was the only one who seemed rested, and I wondered if perhaps the past few weeks had been a blessing in disguise for him.

"We have no time for pleasantries," he began. "Earlier, Helen answered several questions for me regarding the object of Balthasar Brenner's raid earlier today. It is very painful for her to speak so I will communicate the information to you, except when she is the only one capable of answering a question."

I glanced at Helen again, wondering just how much she was suffering. Burn wounds were, I'd heard, some of the most agonizing to endure. Doubtless Solana had arranged to have her fed, and vampires did heal at a faster rate than humans. But what Helen really needed was the blood of a wereshifter. I looked to Constantine, wondering whether he had offered himself or planned to do so, but his expression was inscrutable.

"Brenner removed six vials and a flash drive from the medical vault," Malcolm continued. "These items contained specimens and extensive notes from a series of highly classified experiments involving the vampire parasite."

"What kinds of experiments?" Summers asked, clearly displeased at his own lack of knowledge.

"The research was attempting to create a new, improved strain of parasite—one combining elements from all seven subspecies."

Beside me, Val tensed and leaned forward. "Improved? What the hell do you mean by that?"

The question had exploded from her before she could temper her anger, and I reached for her hand, hoping my touch would prove soothing. I wasn't surprised at her suspicion. Valentine was heavily invested in finding a cure for the vampire parasite—or at least a way to curb its appetite and most detrimental effects—but that priority wasn't shared by most of her colleagues.

"The goal of the project as it has been explained to me," Malcolm said, "was to create a version of the parasite that would combine the strengths of all seven clans while eliminating their weaknesses."

Val shifted restlessly in her chair and muttered something beneath her breath, so quietly that even I couldn't make out the words.

"Was the project a success?" I asked.

Malcolm looked to Helen. When she spoke, I had to lean forward to catch her soft and poorly articulated words. "No. The engineered parasite was a disaster. A cannibal. It would only feed on the blood of other vampires."

"What does that mean?" asked Constantine.

Helen gestured to Solana, who leaned in to catch her words. A frown spread across her face as she listened, and when she finally turned to face the rest of the room, she looked deeply troubled.

"The modified parasite rejected human blood as sustenance and would only accept the blood of vampires who had been infected by one of the original seven strains. The test subjects demonstrated an increase in physical strength and in resistance to sunlight, but their appetites were insatiable. When left unfed, they experienced rapid mental deterioration."

"And now Brenner has this research in his possession?" Fury laced Val's voice. When she leaned heavily back in her chair, I rested my hand on her knee. Beneath my palm her muscles leapt into sharp relief.

I didn't have to guess what she was thinking. A Frankenstein's monster that preyed exclusively on other vampires would be a formidable predator, and if Brenner could produce enough of them, he could conceivably hunt vampires into extinction. Or, if he managed to infect enough vampires at once, he could easily start a civil war.

Malcolm raised one hand in an attempt to forestall an outburst. "Helen has assured me that the cannibal parasite was destroyed, as was the vial containing one subspecies. He may have the notes, but without that seventh vial he cannot duplicate the research."

"Bullshit. All he'd have to do is figure out which parasite he's missing and capture a vampire from that clan."

Helen shook her head and tried to raise herself into a sitting position, only to gasp in pain. She slumped back against the couch as Solana bent over her in concern.

"The synthesis will fail unless the parasite comes from a blood prime," Solana reported a moment later.

"Which strain was destroyed?" asked Foster.

Once again, Solana bent to hear Helen's response. "The vial containing the Sunrunner parasite. After the failed experiment, their blood prime demanded the destruction of her sample."

"Tian?" Val was on her feet, gripping the edge of the table so hard her knuckles turned white. "And you don't think it's a coincidence that Bai was beaten into a bloody pulp? We have to assume Brenner has Tian's location!"

"But how would he have known about the experiments at all?" Constantine's voice was taut, and my panther vibrated at his obvious distress.

"Darren." Summers spat out the traitor's name.

"Darren would never have had access to the research," Foster countered.

"But maybe he saw references somewhere?" I said. "Enough to piece together the gist of the project?"

"Possibly." Malcolm turned his attention to Helen. "I'm aware that Tian is notoriously reclusive. Do you know her current location?"

"No," Solana reported after a brief consultation. "Aside from her retinue, only her second-in-command has that information."

"Which we can assume was tortured out of him by Brenner," Val repeated. She took her seat again, and beneath the table, I pressed my leg against hers in a silent attempt at reassurance.

"Does anyone know Bai's prognosis?" Malcolm asked.

"If there is any change in his condition, Helen will be informed," said Solana.

"There must be something we can do while we wait for him to come out of the coma," I said. "Surely the other members of the delegation must be able to get a message to Tian, even if they don't know where she is."

"And in the meantime, we need to double our efforts to track down Brenner," said Constantine. "If we can determine his movements early enough, we might be able to slow him down or overtake him."

Malcolm rose and began issuing deployment orders. He charged Summers to spearhead the search for Brenner's whereabouts, and asked Foster to work with the Sunrunner delegation to make contact with Tian. He instructed Constantine and me to begin requisitioning personnel and supplies for a raid, and Val to implement a withdrawal freeze at the bank in order to forestall a financial panic.

"Karma and I will see to the security of Headquarters. It must be left well-guarded." He returned his gaze to Helen. "You will remain here to oversee the defenses?"

"Very well." Her unhappiness was clear, even through the rasp of her voice.

Malcolm looked around the room, meeting each of our eyes in turn. "Be prepared to leave at a moment's notice. At the first strong lead on Brenner, we will depart."

CHAPTER NINE

Val grabbed my hand as I turned toward the door. "I need to speak with Solana. Do you want me to meet you at home?"

"I'll stay." I paused, trying to choose my next words carefully. "I know you're upset with Helen, and for good reason. But I don't think Solana is going to be able to—"

Val shook her head. "That's not why I need her help right now. I want to go back up to the lab and get some blood work started so we have a better sense of what the Tear of Isis flower actually does, and why."

"And how long its effects will last," I added, saying what she wouldn't. I could see it flickering in her eyes—the fear that she would descend once again into the emptiness of unmitigated and unquenchable thirst. That her soul would again be lost.

"That, too."

"We'll be okay. No matter what."

Val slid her arms around my waist. "I know." When I tilted my head back to search her eyes, she smiled. "I believe in us more than anything."

I rested my cheek against her chest, trying to soak up each moment of closeness before the inevitable chaos. The feel of her arms around me was nothing short of miraculous. A part of me still couldn't believe she had returned to me from a place that— according to some—was beyond death.

"Toward the end of that meeting, I had a thought," she said into the silence.

"Oh?"

Absently, she smoothed her palms across the small of my back. "The vampire parasite is powerful enough to transform the structure of a person's circulatory system—we know that for sure. But the same must be true of that flower. I can't think of any other way for it to have done what it did to me and to Solana."

"And you think it could be the basis for a cure?"

"Maybe. Or maybe I'm making bad conjectures." A lopsided smile curved her lips. "This wouldn't be the first time over the past two years that I've seen something I can't explain."

"How soon will you know the results of the tests you want to run?"

"Days. But I don't want to waste any time on the front end. We could get called away at any second, and God only knows what will happen then. And who knows—maybe the blood work will reveal something we can use to counteract whatever Brenner's planning."

She looked over my shoulder and I turned to follow her gaze, reluctantly breaking her gentle hold. Solana was conferring with Malcolm as the others filed out the door.

"I'm going to call Tonya," she said quietly. "I don't think the regular Consortium staff can be trusted."

My skin prickled. Tonya had been a physician's assistant of sorts at Consortium Headquarters until a few months ago when Valentine, in a fit of thirst and pique, had turned her. I hated the thought of Val's lips pressed to Tonya's skin, of her cries of abandon as Val stroked and sucked her into oblivion, of Val moving above and inside her.

"Baby, hush, it's okay."

Her words shattered the images cascading before my mind's eye. Only then did I become aware that I was trembling. A nearly subvocal growl vibrated in the back of my throat, and I forced my panther to subside into the depths of my consciousness.

Val rubbed my lower back in slow circles, and I took a few deep breaths as I scanned the room to see if anyone had noticed my lapse. Fortunately, they were all caught up in their own affairs. When Val cupped my face and drew my gaze to hers, I began to apologize.

"No. You have nothing to be sorry for. The only thing I need to know is that you're sure of me now. That you trust me to be true to you. To us."

I rose onto my toes to nip at her chin, then soothed the spot with my lips. "I do."

She searched my eyes, then smiled. "I like the sound of those two words." But before I could reply, she stepped back and raised her phone. "I'll make the call. Will you tell Solana the plan?"

I waited a respectful distance behind Malcolm and caught Solana's attention when he turned for the door. Dark circles shadowed her eyes, and her face was drawn and pale, but the anxiety that had seemed to crackle around her mere hours before had subsided. Our world was in chaos, but deep inside, she was at peace. I could empathize.

"Do you have a few minutes? Val would like to run some blood tests. They shouldn't take long. She's hoping this is the first step in pinning down the biological mechanism of the flower."

Helen opened her eyes briefly, but for once her scrutiny didn't leave me cold. I wondered whether the hell she'd just endured would temper her aggression, or at least her methods. Or perhaps Solana's presence was responsible for the nascent change I felt in her.

"Go," she said to Solana. "You need answers." Her voice was barely audible, even to me. "Please ask Constantine to stay."

Solana brushed the lightest of kisses on Helen's shoulder before joining me. We met Val at the door and headed for the stairwell.

"Thanks for taking the time," Val said as we ascended. The slight note of deference in her voice surprised and gladdened me. I would forever be in debt to Solana, and apparently, Val felt the same.

"What kinds of tests will you run?" asked Solana.

"I want to do a full workup, but that will take a while." Val held the door for us both, and my shoulders tightened at the memory of having been shot in this very hallway only a few hours ago. Battling down both the flashback and my defensive panther, I retraced our earlier steps toward the laboratory.

We rounded the corner to find two pairs of guards flanking the door. All the blood had been cleaned from the floor and walls, and the antiseptic scent burned my nostrils. As we approached, the guards closed ranks, blocking the threshold.

Val halted and crossed her arms beneath her breasts. "Are we going to have a problem, gentlemen?"

One of the vampires, a tall, dark-haired man with a hooked nose, was the one to answer. "We can let you in, Missionary, but two of us must come with you."

A chill ran over me at the sound of Valentine's official title. I still thought of the Missionary as the brute who had turned her and in so doing dramatically changed the course of both our lives.

"Fine. We have one more joining us."

I took the opportunity to check my phone while we waited. I'd missed a call from my mother. Her voice mail message was a rambling monologue about how she missed me and how many feet of snow had fallen in the latest blizzard and was I studying too hard. We were living in two separate worlds, and the disconnect between her questions and my life made me feel a sudden sense of vertigo.

But then Val brushed a light caress across my shoulders, the barest hint of a smile curving her lips when I met her gaze. Even now, acting in an official capacity before perfect strangers, she took the time to make me feel cherished. We had claimed each other in this brave new world, and I could miss my biological family without having to feel utterly adrift.

When Tonya appeared a few minutes later, I was careful to control my voice and expression even as I loosened my hold on my panther ever so slightly. Tonya flinched as she shook my hand, and I knew my nonverbal warning had worked.

"Let's go."

Instead of turning toward the records vault, Val led us down the intersecting corridor in the opposite direction. She paused at a door on the right to enter a code on the security pad attached to the knob. When the guards would have followed her inside, she shook her head.

"This is the only entrance and exit. Stay outside."

The room was a laboratory, complete with workbenches and stainless steel shelves populated by all kinds of equipment. Val went to a drawer and withdrew two syringes, several vials, and a tourniquet.

"I want to run a full battery of tests on these samples," she said as she rolled up her sleeves. "And for what it's worth, I want to take a look right now as well."

"What will you be able to see?" asked Solana.

"The parasite is visible through most microscopes," said Val. "I don't know if I'll be able to tell anything about the effects of the flower, but I do remember what my blood looked like when the parasite was consuming it, so I can make some comparisons." She looked to Tonya. "I'd like you to do a finger stick also, as a control."

Once Tonya had moved on to Solana, I followed Val to the back of the room, where she turned on the largest of the microscopes arranged on the bench. After preparing a slide of her own blood, she bent over the device. I couldn't help but hold my breath, and I had to force myself to think rationally. Even if the flower's effects were already wearing off, that didn't mean I was going to lose Valentine. The Tear of Isis bloomed in thirteen places across the world each month. In the short term, we could harvest it from another location. In the long term, we could try to synthesize it.

Val raised her head, confusion written plainly on her face. "I don't know how to interpret what I'm seeing."

My anxiety spiked and I worked to keep my voice even. "Describe it to me."

"I can make out the parasite floating around in my blood, but it's not all that prevalent. Mostly, I'm seeing something that looks like an altered version of the parasite, but I can't tell what—if anything—it's doing."

"Compare it with mine," Solana said from behind me.

As she examined Solana's sample, Val frowned. "I see more of the free-floating parasite, than in mine, but also those other structures."

"Try mine." Tonya held out a slide.

"Normal," Val said after a moment. She glanced at Solana. "Whatever the flower does, it's expressing differently in each of us."

"That may be related to how we consumed it," said Solana. "It came to you in the blood of a Were whose soul is mated with yours. I can think of no more powerful combination."

Val labeled each of the vials and handed them to Tonya. "Don't take your eyes off these, and run them both through a comprehensive battery of tests, twice. I want to know everything we possibly can about what the flower is doing to our blood cells. When you have the results, call me."

She turned to Solana. "As far as I can see, we don't need to worry about what will happen in the short term. As soon as I know anything more, so will you."

As we left the room and rejoined the guards, I wondered how Solana's conceptualization of her own future had changed over the past few days. Did she want to remain at Helen's side? If so, had she considered willingly making the transition to full vampire so as to join Helen in the darkness? Or did she worry that in losing the light, she would also lose her ability to love? Before hearing their story, I'd believed that an individual needed a soul in order to feel and express that kind of devotion. Now, I wasn't so sure. Even during our separation, Valentine had fixated on me obsessively. Could she have learned a measure of compassion over time?

In my musings, I had fallen behind Val and Solana. Shaking my head, I picked up my pace and forced myself not to dwell on the repercussions of whatever complex processes were going on in Valentine's circulatory system. Until she received the test results, we all needed to focus instead on the very real possibility that any minute, we would learn news of Brenner's location. We had to prepare for every contingency and be ready to deploy at a moment's notice.

❖

An hour later, I threw open the doors to Valentine's wardrobe, wondering where to start. While she returned to the bank to act on

Malcolm's orders, I had gone to the apartment to pack. Two large duffle bags stood near the door: one filled with cold weather gear and the other with lighter clothing. Now I surveyed Val's gun collection. Doubtless, she would want to make her own choices about weaponry, but on the off chance that we received word before she returned home, I wanted to be ready.

I was just reaching for the largest of her sniper rifles when the door opened. As soon as I saw her face, I knew she hadn't heard any good news. She pulled me into the living room and sat heavily on the couch. I curled into her and slipped one hand beneath her shirt to rub her taut abdominal muscles.

"What's happened, sweetheart?"

"Not any one thing. More like a confluence of events." She leaned her head back and stared at the ceiling. "Blaine is escalating quickly, and Caleb has yet to find any vulnerabilities that we can easily capitalize on. Though his people did uncover a possible connection to the drug trade."

"Blaine might be the one managing it?"

"Yes. Though it's still unclear whether he's always had that role, or if this is something new."

The fatigue in her voice made my heart ache. I straddled her thighs and combed my fingers through her hair, hoping to help her relax. "I take it his political connections are throwing up all kinds of road blocks?"

"Like you wouldn't believe." When my massaging touch reached the back of her neck, she sighed in pleasure. "To top it off, there's still no word from Tian, and Summers's people haven't found any reliable leads as to Brenner's whereabouts."

I made my touch firmer in the hopes of distracting her. A breathy moan escaped her lips as I found a knot above her left shoulder, and the sound galvanized my desire. The urgency of the moment crystallized: we might have only minutes before we were called to action, and it might be days or weeks before we could be close again.

I needed her. Now. Pulling back, I whipped off my shirt, gratified to see her instinctively raise her hands to cup my breasts.

"No." I slapped her hands away, and before she could protest, I pressed my right nipple into her mouth. She groaned against my skin, the hot swipes of her tongue electrifying me. The short, sharp thrusts of her hips were proof of her own arousal and I returned my grip to her hair, pulling her even closer.

The world disappeared as we moved together. When the ache between my thighs intensified, I unbuttoned my pants and guided her hand inside. My head snapped back in unbearable pleasure as she filled me, and I moaned her name between gritted teeth. Yanking her head away from my breast, I braced myself against the couch and rode her fingers slowly. She kept her hand still and let me set the pace. When I looked down into her eyes, she licked her lips.

"So hot, baby. I love you, and you are so, so fucking hot."

I leaned in, exposing my neck. "Drink."

She lunged for me, thrusting deep with her fingers as her teeth broke my skin. Ecstasy burst through my veins, dimming my vision as my body flowed for her, around her. Distantly, I felt her shudder against me and rejoiced that she too had found release.

Minutes passed before I could move. Finally, I pushed myself up, allowing Val to ease her fingers from my body. She stared at me in awe.

"What *was* that?"

I stroked the damp hair back from her forehead. "Us, my love. That was us."

"We are awesome."

My laughter caught me by surprise, and it felt so good. That was exactly the kind of sentiment I'd fallen in love with Valentine over. Despite her strained relationship with her family, despite having been turned into a vampire, Val had never lost her childlike exuberance until she had lost her soul. To see that radiant enthusiasm reappear in the wake of all she had been through over the past few months felt like a miracle.

"I love you so much." I kissed her slowly, gently, enjoying the gradual build of heat between us.

And then, just as I was entertaining the thought of dragging her to bed, my phone vibrated. While my first instinct was to ignore it,

I knew I couldn't. Reluctantly, I leaned back just far enough to fish my cell phone out of my pocket. I had expected Karma or Solana— maybe even Constantine.

"It's Olivia," I said, hearing the surprise in my voice.

"Really." Val cupped my waist, her thumbs sliding along my rib cage. I wondered whether she had any sense of her own possessiveness or whether, like my own, it was instinctual. "What does she want?"

"To know if I'm still awake." I tapped out a simple *Yes*, in response.

Her reply came only seconds later. *Me too. Can't sleep. Is there anything I can do?*

I sat back on Val's legs and turned the phone to face her. "Sounds like she's having a hard time dealing with everything she knows. She wants to help."

I wasn't surprised. Olivia had learned the truth about wereshifters while dating one, and she'd practically blackmailed me into taking her along on my mission to find the Tear of Isis. Since my success in reclaiming Valentine, she'd had no role to play.

"Maybe she can," said Val.

"How? No one at the Consortium will trust her."

"But I do." Val smiled wryly. She and Olivia had known each other since childhood. They were too alike not to be competitors, but the lengths to which Olivia had gone on my behalf had clearly impressed Val despite the fact that Olivia wanted me.

"If I asked her to go after Blaine, she might actually make some headway."

I considered her idea. Olivia's family had even more powerful political connections than did Val's, and her work in the district attorney's office must have opened up even more avenues.

"Shall I tell her to come over?"

Val nodded. "We can finish packing in the meantime."

Twenty minutes later, Val was just zipping up the bag containing her weapons and spare ammunition when the buzzer announced Olivia's arrival downstairs. As we waited for her to make the elevator ride up, Val pulled me close to her and grinned.

"My fingers still smell like you."

I tugged her head down for a quick, hard kiss. "Good. I'm yours. So no need to vamp out on her."

Val was still laughing when the door chimed. As she stepped forward to kiss Olivia on the cheek, I couldn't help but compare them. Olivia, dressed in slimming jeans and a fitted, v-neck black sweater, was undeniably attractive. But only Val, who had changed into a white A-shirt and dark cargo pants, exuded a coiled strength and confidence that rekindled my desire. She moved aside and I hugged Olivia briefly. Always slim, she was even thinner than she had been a few days ago. Her shoulders were slightly hunched, as though they carried an invisible weight.

"Are you doing okay, Liv?"

"Fine, thanks." The response was automatic, and she seemed to be having a hard time looking directly at all of us. And then she noticed the bags stacked to one side of the hallway. "Traveling somewhere?"

"We're going after Brenner as soon as we get a lead." Val gestured toward the kitchen. "Want a drink?"

"Sure. Something strong."

As she mixed a martini, Val explained the situation at the Bank of Mithras. "My people are looking into ways to counter Blaine's lawsuits, but we're also hoping to go on offense against him. Tonight, my head of security received information suggesting that Blaine may be ultimately responsible for Brenner's drug-peddling operations in the city. Would you be interested in investigating?"

Olivia's eyes lit up and she squared her shoulders. "Very much, yes."

"I'll make sure you can liaise with the bank," continued Val. "But it would be best if you used your own resources. I'll compensate you, of course."

"That's fine."

I could tell that her brain was already going a mile a minute. The cloak of her fatigue had suddenly been replaced by a hunter's air of determination.

"Promise us you won't go rushing into anything," I said. "This isn't the drug trade you're used to fighting."

"I'll be careful," she said, but the reply was perfunctory.

Val picked up her phone. "Caleb," she said a moment later. "I've just asked Olivia Lloyd to work the drug angle. She's going to use her own people, but if you come across anything helpful, I want you to send it her way."

She listened for a moment, then asked Olivia for her cell number and repeated it to Caleb. Suddenly, she stiffened.

"I have another call incoming. Headquarters. Call you back." Her gaze held mine as she switched over. "Darrow." When the barest hint of a smile curved her lips, I knew we'd finally heard some good news.

"We'll be there. Half an hour, tops." She hung up the phone, already in motion toward the hall. "Time to go."

Olivia threw back her drink as Val opened the door for her. "Will I be able to contact you if I have questions or information?" she asked.

"Calls only. Don't leave a message, and you'll need to memorize the number I'm about to give you. It's for my satellite phone." She rattled off a string of digits. "Okay?"

"Great." Olivia stepped across the threshold, looking between us. "Be careful."

"Careful as we can be." Val shut the door, then faced me. "Tian got a message through to Headquarters. She was in Vancouver and is on the move north and east. She'll relay more information when she has a chance."

"So, cold weather gear." I slipped on my heavy boots and grabbed the larger of the duffels. "Canada. Interesting. I thought she would be somewhere in China."

Val handed me my parka, tucked hers under her arm, and hefted the bag full of guns. "That's probably why she wasn't."

The door swung shut behind us, and at the hollow click of the lock I wondered how long it would be before we could return. We both sorely needed some peace in our lives, but as long as we were together, I could easily forgo other kinds of stability.

valentine

CHAPTER TEN

The jet, with its leather seats, booths, full-service kitchen, and private conference room, was even more luxurious than my father's. Heavy blackout curtains had been tacked down over each of the oval windows for the sake of Foster and Summers.

I spent the first hour of the flight corresponding with Bridget, whom I'd left in control of the bank. She would do a good job—better than me, probably. Depending on her performance, perhaps I could make her the permanent CEO when I returned. Despite having developed an appreciation for the banking profession over the past few months, there was so much I wanted to accomplish that had nothing to do with the world of high finance. In particular, I was fascinated by the Tear of Isis and its restorative properties. If I could study the flower in-depth, I might be able to isolate and synthesize the components that caused such miraculous effects. Becoming a vampire would no longer mean being sentenced to darkness for eternity.

I couldn't think of the flower without being reminded of the Herculean effort Alexa had undertaken for me. For us. After getting caught up with Karma during the first half of the flight, she had fallen asleep with her head pillowed on my shoulder. Her slow, even breaths puffed against my neck, and as I let myself follow her example, I silently vowed to make the most of this second chance she'd given us.

When the pilot announced that we were just under an hour from touching down, Malcolm summoned us into the conference room, where he gave Foster the floor.

"Our latest update from Tian indicates that she initially made a feint toward Calgary but is in fact heading north to Prince George. If we fly directly there, we risk alerting Brenner to her plans. Instead, we will land at our original destination just outside of Vancouver and drive the remainder of the way.

"We'll split into two groups. Both will begin by traveling northeast, reinforcing Tian's deception. One group will then swing up and around to approach Prince George from the west, while the other maintains an easterly route."

"What's the next step?" Alexa asked.

"We escort her to New York," said Malcolm.

"Leon, Malcolm, and Constantine will take the eastern path," said Foster. "Val, Alexa, Karma, and I will circle west."

The four of us spent the remainder of the flight in one of the booths, hunched over the table with several maps of British Columbia spread out before us. North of Vancouver, the countryside quickly became mountainous and heavily forested—ideal terrain for an ambush. While it seemed likely that the majority of Brenner's forces in the region would be targeting Tian, I had no doubt that he was also monitoring our movements.

When we landed at a small, private airfield outside the city limits, we found two black Humvees parked just inside the hangar. Several boxes of combat gear and survival supplies had been stacked between them.

"Help yourselves to the equipment," said Malcolm, "and be sure to take a box of provisions as well."

My breath steamed in the cold air as I pulled on a ballistic vest over my sweater. The side pockets yielded MREs, a knife, and several packets of caffeine pills and painkillers. The boxes contained additional medical supplies and food rations. I muscled one into the trunk of the nearest Humvee and turned to the sight of Alexa tightening the fit of her vest. Her dark hair brushed gently against her shoulders and her lower lip stuck out ever so slightly in a frown of concentration and the barest flicker of her abdominal muscles was visible as she wrestled to adjust one shoulder strap.

Love and thirst flared up together, twin fires curling around my heart, galvanizing it into action. Despite the urgency of the moment, I stepped forward, stilling her hands and untangling the twisted strap.

"There." And then I kissed her, right there in front of everyone—a deep, searching kiss that stole my breath and hers. Color rushed to her cheeks when I pulled back, but she kept her eyes on me and didn't turn away until I bent to grab one of our duffels.

As we loaded our bags into the trunks, the inevitable argument began.

"Who's driving?" asked Karma.

"I am," Foster and I said simultaneously.

For a moment, we squared off across the glossy hood. A few feet away, Summers and Constantine appeared to be engaged in a similar battle.

"Maybe you should arm wrestle," Alexa suggested dryly.

"This is a waste of time," I said. "And we don't have any of that to spare. You take the first shift. I'm going to play with my guns in the backseat."

Karma and Alexa laughed, and even Foster cracked a half-grin. For an instant, I felt a strange sense of disconnect—as though we were simply four friends about to pile into a car for a road trip, instead of four creatures of legend and nightmare about to attempt a daring rescue. And then I felt the weight of my bulletproof vest bearing down on my shoulders, and the moment passed.

"Check in every hour," Constantine called as we climbed into the vehicle.

As Foster revved the engine, I moved the bag containing our weapons to the space between Alexa and me on the backseat. Karma served as navigator while I pieced together my sniper rifle and Alexa loaded the shotguns and pistols. Her western Wisconsin upbringing had given her a comfort level with firearms that I hadn't managed to achieve until recently.

Our task completed, we distributed the weapons and settled in for the long haul. The drive would take just over ten hours, and it was imperative that we reach Tian before the sun rose. We had very little leeway, and we had to push hard.

The Humvee's engine roared in our ears, making all but the most necessary conversation impossible between the front and back seats. Alexa curled up with her back against my side, allowing both of us to remain vigilant even as we stayed in close contact. The forested landscape outside the windows passed in a dark blur broken only occasionally by the ghostly reach of the moonlight.

Several hours into the journey, Alexa lifted my right hand and pressed her lips to my knuckles. "I think we should buy a home in the country."

I smiled, daring to glance at her for just a moment before returning my attention to the night. "Tell me more. I want to be able to see the picture in your head."

"There are several," she said, barely audible above the throbbing engine. "Sometimes I think of a large house on its own mountain in Vermont or New Hampshire. Other times, I see a smaller home on the coast. Massachusetts, maybe, or Maine."

"We could combine those visions if we bought a mountainous island."

She laughed. "We have more money than I'd ever dreamed of, but not enough to purchase an island."

"Not yet," I conceded. "But we will. We will, baby."

When she let out a quiet sigh of contentment and shifted against me, I felt my heart expand as though it were a balloon. Before Alexa, my life had been a constant battle—against my family, my expectations, and sometimes even myself. She granted me a measure of serenity I'd barely known to hope for. Even now, with the very pillars of our world in jeopardy of destruction, the core of my soul knew only peace.

My satphone rang. As the call connected, the sound of gunfire pierced my ear. Heart suddenly thundering in my chest, I shouted for Foster to pull over.

"Val!" Summers's voice was labored. "Ran into Brenner's scouts. Car totaled. In a firefight."

"Stay put! We're coming to get you."

"Don't—"

The call went dead, swallowing whatever he had been about to say. "Summers? Summers! Damn it!"

"Tell me their position," Karma said, her voice eerily calm as she struggled to keep her jackal from reacting to the emotional moment.

I read off the coordinates logged by the phone. As she keyed them into the GPS, I double-checked the readiness of my pistol before stuffing it into my waistband.

"We can be there inside half an hour," Karma said. "Maybe less. Devon, you'll want to keep on this road to—"

"Wait," Foster cut in. "Are we sure we should go charging into this? Didn't I hear Leon say 'don't' before the connection broke off?"

"We have no idea what else he was going to say," said Alexa. "But our first commitment is to Tian and the mission."

I handed my shotgun to Alexa, threw off my seat belt, and opened the door. "We are not leaving them to fend for themselves. Get the fuck out of that seat. I'm driving."

Displeasure was written in every line of Foster's face, but she obeyed. "If this goes to shit, Val, I'm holding you responsible."

"Works for me."

No sooner had the back door closed behind her than we were in motion. I pushed the vehicle to its limits, swerving around hairpin curves and accelerating down steep slopes, capitalizing on our momentum.

With less than a mile to go, I checked my seat belt. "Choose your targets carefully," I shouted over the engine's whine. "The scene could be a mess."

"One thousand feet," said Karma as we made a steep, winding ascent. "Seven fifty."

The throb of the engine eased as we crested the slope. I kept the accelerator fully depressed, and we rocketed down the far side.

"Lean right!" We careened into an S-turn, and I felt the car lift onto two wheels for several breathtaking seconds before finally crashing back to earth. And then, quite suddenly, we were upon them.

The other Humvee had somehow turned onto its side and was dangling precariously off a steep embankment to the right, just a hundred feet ahead. Gunfire arced between it and two Jeeps blocking the road.

"Brace!"

Allowing instinct to guide me, I braked hard and swerved, sending the car into a dizzying series of rotations. When its back fender broadsided one Jeep and sent it tumbling off the road, satisfaction trumped the bolts of agony that shot up my arms and into my shoulders. As soon as our car came to rest, I threw open the door and somersaulted out, flowing back onto my feet without a hitch. I zigged and zagged in an effort to stay out of the line of fire, but my footprints were easily traceable. No sooner had I pressed my back to a large tree for cover than the hollow thunk of bullets into bark erupted all around me. At least I was drawing their fire. If they were focused on me, Alexa would be safe. She would also be dangerous.

I closed my eyes to heighten my hearing. Weres made very little noise even in human form, but the quiet snap of a twig and the soft rustle of undergrowth to my left might not simply be the night air. Holding my breath, hands closed around the grip of my firearm, I waited for my adversary to make another move.

The dull thud of deadweight impacting snow brought the darkness alight with renewed gunfire. I spun toward the sound and shot one of Brenner's soldiers in the head as he raised his own weapon to fire at Alexa. Jaws bloodied, she stood atop the body of another man, his neck bent at an impossible angle. Our gazes locked for one inexpressible moment before she bent to satisfy her hunger.

I watched over her while she fed, combing the surrounding woods for any sign of attack. Despite the visibility of our most recent battle, I sensed no reinforcements. Once Alexa had finished, we slowly worked our way back toward the vehicles, darting from tree to tree. As we finally reached the road, Karma and Constantine, both in human form, stepped out in front of the tilted Humvee and began debating whether it could make the rest of the trip.

My first instinct was to force them back under cover. If any of Brenner's scouts were still lurking in the darkness, Karma and Constantine risked getting picked off. And then I realized they had positioned themselves as bait.

I gestured to Alexa to move left while I went right and then picked my way slowly across the frozen landscape, alert to the smallest sign of disruption. A gust of wind made the pine needles rustle like bones. Several feet away, a thin layer of snow fell from an overburdened branch.

Suddenly, a black blur whizzed past me only to be brought up short by the throaty report of a shotgun. Blood fountained into the air, warm and metallic, burning through the snow as it fell. I ran forward toward the shooter, pistol extended, giving voice to the scream of rage that welled up in my throat. He died quickly, and I collapsed to the ground beside Alexa. She had seen him. She had saved me.

The shell had ripped into her chest, but even as her heartbeat faltered, her body blurred. She emerged into human form naked, gasping, curled in a pool of her own gore. Almost immediately, her teeth began to chatter.

I slipped one arm under her neck and the other beneath her knees, heedless of everything but the need to keep her safe.

CHAPTER ELEVEN

My brain had split in two. As I emerged onto the road, part of me remembered to call out "Clear," and "I need a blanket," even as fear and anger and the need for vengeance curdled in my gut.

I knew the moment Karma and Constantine scented all the blood. Karma gasped. Constantine took a step toward me.

"Is she all right?"

Karma ran for the back of our Humvee, and I heard warped hinges protest as she opened the trunk. Moments later, she spread out a blanket on the ground at my feet. I lowered Alexa down to it as carefully as if she were made of glass, then cupped the side of her face with the hand that wasn't covered in her blood. She blinked up at me, her breaths coming fast and shallow. I wanted to bury my fist into the asphalt. Why did she look so dazed? Why wasn't she speaking?

"Val." Karma rested a hand between my shoulder blades. "Tell me what happened."

"She was shot in the heart." My voice snarled on another surge of fury. "Her pulse…I felt it falter. She was almost gone, and then she shifted."

Constantine crouched next to us. "Sometimes, when a transformation is motivated by extreme trauma, there's a bit of shell shock afterward." He uncorked his canteen and pulled an energy bar out of one vest pocket. "May I?"

I nodded and he gently slipped his hand behind her head, raising her into a sitting position. When he tilted the canteen against her lips, she sipped at the water. That small, simple movement sent relief cascading through so sharply that my breath caught.

Karma leaned in close. "You're covered in her blood, Val," she whispered. "Go change. We'll get her to eat something, too. She'll recover quickly."

I didn't want to let her out of my sight, but neither did I want to remind her of the trauma she'd just endured. Forcing my legs into motion, I backed away from the blanket and hurried to our vehicle. Across the road, Malcolm, Summers, and Foster were trying to right the second Humvee. Without a care for modesty, I stripped, rolled my soiled clothes into a bundle, and scrubbed myself quickly with clean snow. My skin grew taut and pebbled, but I didn't feel the chill.

As the signs of Alexa's near-death experience melted onto the pavement, her voice pierced the night like a lighthouse beacon. I dressed quickly and hurried back to the blanket, where Karma was helping her into new clothes. When she saw me, she closed the distance between us with no regard for her bare feet. I cradled her face in my hands and kissed her tenderly.

"That was too close. How are you feeling?"

"I'm okay," she said, palms stroking over my shoulders. "A little shaken up at first, but that's passed."

I pulled her close, resting my cheek against her silky hair. "You saved my life. Again."

"I didn't mean to frighten you," she murmured against my clean vest. "It was instinctive. You would have done the same thing."

For a long moment I blocked everything out—the biting cold, Summers hurling invectives at the Humvee, the urgency of our mission. Alexa was alive and in my arms, her heartbeat synced with mine.

"We need to move," Malcolm ordered, breaking my reverie. "The Humvee is a lost cause. We'll take their operational Jeep."

While Alexa laced up a new pair of boots, I joined the small group transferring our supplies between vehicles. Within minutes, we were ready to leave. I glanced at my watch, steeling myself for the tense hours ahead as we tried to outrun the daylight.

Malcolm shared my sense of urgency. "Stay together. The Jeep will lead. If we push hard, we can arrive before sunrise."

Foster didn't argue when I took the wheel, and Karma conceded the passenger's side to Alexa. I set a blistering pace away from the scene of the shootout, channeling my leftover adrenaline into navigating the sharp curves of the mountain road at top speed. Whenever I could, I rested one hand on Alexa's knee. Anchoring myself.

The Jeep was much quieter than the Humvee had been, and as we drew closer to Prince George without further mishaps, the conversation turned to the object of our quest. Rumors abounded about Tian, Blood Prime of the Sunrunners—the largest and arguably most powerful vampire clan.

"How old is she?" Karma asked. "Does anyone actually know?"

"Rumor has it she's the oldest vampire alive," said Foster. "But no one except her most trusted servants knows anything for certain."

"Even Helen has never met her," I chimed in.

"Really?" Alexa sounded shocked, and Karma's expression mirrored her tone.

For the majority of us, Helen Lambros epitomized power and success. She oversaw the most important district of the Consortium and had charge of the Order of Mithras. Over two-hundred years old, she commanded the respect of her peers around the world. And yet, she had never been invited to a face-to-face with Tian.

"You had quite a few dealings with her lieutenant, didn't you, Val?" asked Foster.

"Bai. Yes." I saw again the motionless form on the stretcher—shoulders dislocated, ribs a mass of bruises, face beaten to a bloody pulp. Brenner's soldiers had not been merciful. They had delivered him alive, but without immediate medical intervention, he would have certainly died within hours.

"What's he like?" asked Karma. "Did you learn anything more about Tian from him?"

I thought back to my business transactions with Bai. We had only met twice, once in my office at the bank and once in my suite at

Tartarus. He had been an impressive negotiator, but never once had his professional façade slipped—except to betray the impersonal and unrelenting thirst that was the shared legacy of all vampires.

"Charismatic, but cold. A shrewd businessman. Accustomed to getting what he wants."

"It sounds like he learned from the best," said Alexa.

Silence descended then, and I glanced at the clock to find that it was past five o'clock in the morning. Sunrise was just over an hour away.

I smoothed my palm over Alexa's thigh to get her attention. "Will you call Malcolm to confirm Tian's coordinates? And then let's go over the route a few times."

I didn't say what I was thinking—that there could be no mistakes now. One wrong turn might mean the difference between life and death for Foster. I glanced at her in the rearview mirror, but she looked out on the gradually brightening sky with an inscrutable expression. I reached for Alexa's hand and squeezed it briefly, hoping she could understand just how thankful I was to be able to watch the day dawn with joy and not despair.

After exchanging a few words over the satellite phone, Alexa began to punch numbers into her GPS.

"No change. Malcolm says she's settling in for daylight. The safe house is in the suburbs, south and west of Prince George."

The road led us down out of the mountains into a wide valley, where signs of human life became more and more prevalent. I eased off the accelerator. The last thing we wanted to do was attract the attention of local law enforcement.

Prince George, Alexa informed us as she read from the GPS, lay at the junction of two mountain ranges and two rivers. Right now, the latter were most likely frozen.

"Maybe we should come back for a ski vacation," I said. "You know, when we're not so preoccupied."

Alexa laughed. Karma smiled and shook her head. Foster didn't react. Her entire being was focused on the east. Nothing I said or did would be able to distract her from the dread that welled up in each altered cell of her body.

I turned from the highway onto a sinuous country road running parallel to one tributary of the river. Houses sprang up more and more frequently, punctuated by restaurants, general stores, and small shopping centers. Alexa directed us into a neighborhood where the homes looked as though they'd been stamped out by a cookie cutter. Nondescript boxes covered by steep roofs—a testament to how heavy the snow could be, I guessed—they only varied in the color of siding, trim, and shutters.

"This reminds me of my hometown," said Alexa.

Karma reached forward to squeeze her shoulder. "This reminds *me* of Jersey."

Tension trumped my urge to laugh at her wisecrack. We scanned the streets for any sign that Brenner's soldiers had managed to head us off or track down Tian's location, but on the surface at least, everything seemed normal. Slowly, the neighborhood was coming to life in preparation for the new day. Lights were just flickering on in several houses, and a few early-risers were out collecting their newspapers or warming up their cars. One man walking his dog stopped to scrutinize us as we passed, but his attention wasn't prolonged.

"Caravanning with a Humvee isn't exactly helping us keep a low profile," I said.

"It would be much worse if we weren't in northern Canada." Karma pointed to several of the driveways ahead, where trucks and Jeeps were in high supply. "We won't stand out too much."

As I turned onto a cul-de-sac, Alexa pointed straight ahead. "That's the one."

The house was beige, its shutters and door crimson. A minivan, windows rimed with frost, stood in the driveway. I pulled alongside the curb and turned off the engine.

"You're sure."

Alexa glanced from the GPS to the house and back again. "Positive."

I glanced at my watch. Ten minutes until sunrise. If we were wrong, or if this was a trap, Foster and Summers would pay the ultimate price. No one had emerged from the vehicle behind us, so I took the initiative. As I stepped onto the driveway, I positioned the car door as a shield between my body and the house while I scanned its windows for any sign of a weapon.

"Looks quiet," Alexa said as she joined me.

And then the garage door opened. Alexa at my side, I moved forward just far enough to see inside. Clean swept and empty save for a set of shelves at the back holding several boxes, it didn't look like a hideout—which was, of course, the point. Neither did the tall man who stood in the entrance look the part of a servant of the most powerful vampire in the world. He wore a faded pair of jeans and a dark sweater, and he beckoned urgently to us.

"Inside," he hissed. "Quickly."

"Babe?" I knew she could tell his species by scent.

"He's human."

Of the humans who were aware of the existence of vampires and wereshifters, some had allied with the Consortium and some against. I couldn't help feeling suspicious, but we were running out of options.

Glancing over my shoulder, I saw that the occupants of the other car had formed a loose semicircle behind us. At Malcolm's nod, we joined the man inside the garage. He shut the door immediately and drew a thick dark curtain across its windows. Foster's eyes closed briefly, her shoulders loosening in relief.

"Too fucking close," muttered Summers.

"I am Jonah," the man said. "One of Lady Tian's personal servants." He withdrew a small rectangular device from his pocket. "Before I can allow you to enter, your identity must be verified."

The portable fingerprint device worked quickly, and within a few minutes, Jonah was leading us into the kitchen. It looked exactly as I had expected—medium-grade appliances, linoleum tiling, and faux-marble counters. A chrome-plated teakettle was steaming on the stove, and the scent of garlic and soy sauce lingered in the air.

As we crossed into the living room, I had to suppress the urge to ask whether I should remove my shoes. Old habits die hard, and my mother had trained me well in social niceties. A fire had been kindled in the hearth, and between its light and several tall lamps, the room was bright despite the drawn curtains.

A woman sat in an armchair before the fireplace, her back to the flames. Sharp cheekbones stood out from a heart-shaped face as smooth as a child's. Whether she had been turned in her teens or early twenties was impossible to tell. The chair nearly swallowed her diminutive frame, but the aura of power radiating from her more than compensated for her petite stature. Two female guards flanked Tian. Like Jonah and their mistress, they were dressed casually— presumably to fit in with the suburban environment—but assault rifles were strapped to their backs and I was sure they carried more weapons in concealment.

Jonah introduced each of us in turn. He saved me for last, and I wondered if he was trying to figure out the proper way to go about it. I held two separate titles—positions that had fallen to me by default. To my knowledge, no one had ever been both.

"And finally, Valentine Darrow, the Missionary and Blood Prime."

I stepped forward as the others had done and greeted Tian with a short, crisp bow. But when I would have rejoined Alexa, Tian gestured for me to move closer. As I approached, I found myself strangely mesmerized by her eyes. A lustrous, sapphire blue, they seemed to see far beyond the appearance I presented to the world. Under the intensity of her gaze I felt split open, peeled back, dissected.

"You are the object of extraordinary rumors, Valentine." Her voice was soprano and melodic—pure, like the chime of a bell. "And now, it appears they are true."

"To which rumors do you refer, Lady?"

She laughed. "There is no need to be so formal," she said. "You and I are peers, after all. And you needn't be coy, either."

I inclined my head but kept silent, remembering the old adage about the perils of making assumptions. After several seconds of silence, she smiled.

"I see you are cautious. The rumors left that out." She stood and paced around me in a tight circle. "You made your transition, became a full vampire. And yet, now you are able to walk under the sun." She stopped in front of me, craning her neck to meet my eyes. "This is true?"

Without breaking eye contact, I extended my arm backward. A moment later, Alexa's fingers brushed against mine as she took the cue to join me.

"It's true, yes. All thanks to Alexa. She has saved my life many times—most recently, just hours ago. And she also saved my soul."

Tian looked between us, a half-smile curving her lips. "We will speak more of this. But not now." She returned to the chair, her gaze taking in all of us at once. "Your vehicles must be moved, in case Brenner is scouting by air. Jonah will show you where they can be concealed. Two rooms upstairs have been prepared for you, if you wish to rest." She focused in on Malcolm. "You and I should retire to the office, where we can discuss our plans for this evening. We will all reconvene at noon."

As Tian's guards escorted them out of the room, Karma touched my shoulder to get my attention.

"Constantine and I will move the cars. You two should get some rest."

Karma's generosity was touching, and I smiled in gratitude. Now that we had reached relative safety, fatigue was creeping in around the edges of my brain like a fog. I needed to sleep for about four days, but in the meantime, I would gladly take the four hours Tian was offering.

"Thank you. We owe you one."

I tugged at Alexa's hand, drawing her down the hallway and up the L-shaped staircase. We claimed the first empty room we came to, which held two full-sized beds. I closed the door, shucked off my boots and vest, and collapsed on the one closer to the window. Turning to face Alexa, I opened my arms. She smiled—an open, wholehearted smile that had always been mine.

"If only 'Lady Tian' could see you now," she said, dropping her own outer layers to the floor.

"Well, she can't. This is only for you."

She slid into my embrace and I buried my face in the curve of her neck, breathing in deeply. Her scent never failed to inflame my thirst, but in this moment my need to hold her close trumped my urge to take her. I slid my hands beneath her shirt to massage the taut muscles of her back, and the sensation of her warm skin against my fingertips at once stirred my passion and soothed the anxiety that had lingered after her close call in the forest.

"Speaking of Tian," I said, "what did you think of her?"

She pulled back just far enough to look into my eyes. "She's surprisingly tiny."

I muffled my laughter against her shoulder. "So was Napoleon."

"Point taken." She combed her fingers through my hair and I reveled in the perfect fit of our bodies, even through two layers of clothes. "You should drink, my love."

I shook my head. "Not right now. Maybe later, before we leave."

"But—"

I cupped her cheek with my free hand. "You almost died today, Alexa. That was *close*. You know it was. For a second, it felt like… like when you had the virus."

She shivered lightly and her gaze turned inward. I would never be able to know what she had experienced in those terrifying seconds after her human body had failed but before her panther had emerged victorious over death. I only knew that in the aftermath of my own terror, I needed to nurture and strengthen her. There would be time for me to claim her blood after she had rested.

"I love you," I whispered against her temple. "I need you. Only you. You believe that, right?"

Alexa blinked, snapping out of whatever dark memory had held her. "My faith in us is the cornerstone of every other belief." She kissed me gently, then turned onto her side and drew my arm across her breasts. "Sleep well, sweetheart. See you in my dreams."

CHAPTER TWELVE

I woke three hours later, just shy of eleven o'clock. At first, I resisted alertness, hoping that Alexa's rhythmic breathing would pull me back into slumber. But as the minutes passed, my brain kicked into hyperdrive. The nap had taken the edge off my exhaustion and now I needed to be in motion.

Slipping out of bed without Alexa's knowledge wouldn't normally have been possible, but I suspected her energy had been much more depleted than either of us realized. I moved quietly around the other bed where Karma had decided to crash and stopped in the bathroom for a quick shower before heading downstairs.

The last person I'd expected to see in the kitchen was Tian, but there she was, sitting at the wooden kitchen table, hands clasped around a ceramic mug. Dressed entirely in black, she was already prepared for the evening's mission. Her ever-vigilant guards were leaning against the wall behind her, but they straightened as I entered.

"Valentine." Her once-over made me feel disheveled, as though I'd had a choice about wearing the same clothes she'd seen me in earlier. "Join me. Would you like some tea?"

"Please."

She clapped her hands and Jonah immediately appeared in the kitchen doorway. "Tea for our guest please, Jonah."

The steam rising off the dark liquid was fragrant with the scent of chrysanthemum, and I inhaled it deeply. Tian's scrutiny was palpable, but I refused to let her rattle me. We were, as she had said, peers. And I would act like one.

"Will you answer a question for me?" said Tian.

"Probably."

A smile flashed across her lips. "Your lack of pretense is refreshing, but rest assured, I am not asking you to reveal clan secrets. This question is one I have asked many times, of many individuals, over hundreds of years. I would like to know your experience of the sunlight. The details of how it feels to you."

I frowned in confusion. "But surely you've felt it recently?"

"Not for centuries."

"So long? You could survive with impunity for several seconds, possibly even a full minute."

Tian sat back in her chair, tracing patterns through the ring of moisture her mug had left on the table. "When I was a child, my favorite haunt was a small pond on my family's estate. In the spring and summer, lotus blossoms bloomed so abundantly that the water was no longer visible. I used to sit by the pond for hours, luxuriating in the warmth of the sun on my neck, my shoulders. Each freckle, my father told me, was a kiss from the light. My mother, who wanted my skin to remain porcelain white, tried to forbid me to go. But he was indulgent.

"You are quite right, Valentine, that my body could endure the sun—however briefly. Any physical pain would be well worth the experience. But it is my mind and my heart that I do not trust. A recovered addict cannot sip their poison. So, I fear, it would be with me."

Her voice was thick with nostalgia that prompted both my sympathy and empathy. "Why do you want me to remind you of what you've lost?"

She smiled sadly. "To remember the sun is to remember humanity."

The answer shocked me. I had never heard Helen speak this way. She had exhibited brief moments of nostalgia in my presence, but never the kind of soulful regret with which Tian spoke now. Helen embraced the chill she had found in the darkness—the distance between herself and mortality.

"You seem surprised," Tian said.

"I am, a little. What is it about humanity that you find so important to remember?"

Tian turned her gaze to the blacked out window, as though she could see the sun-drenched world beyond. "Unlike wereshifters, we cannot be born. We can only be made. Humans are our raw materials. We come from them, and to deny their influence on us is to deny an integral part of ourselves."

Her eyes met mine, and I was helpless to look away. "I reflect on the human experience because doing so makes me a stronger ruler. As powerful as we are, humans still control most of the world. To forget that, and to forget how life feels to them, would be myopic."

I sat back in my chair, uncertain of how to reply. Most of my peers regarded humans as weak and vulnerable. As prey. Tian's perspective was remarkable, and hearing her insights made me want to share something in return. The least I could do was to answer her original question.

"After Alexa…brought me back," I began, "I was so confused. Disoriented. My psychology, my emotions, were out of sync with my memories. Every new feeling threatened to overwhelm me.

"We were in my apartment, talking. I was struggling to process everything that had just happened. The day was overcast, and in my confusion I didn't realize the curtains had been drawn back. Suddenly, the sun broke through the clouds and streamed into the room, illuminating everything. As though some deity had plunged the world into gold leaf.

"I was terrified beyond all reason. I cowered in the light. But Alexa knelt beside me and reminded me that I was whole again. That I had nothing to fear. She coaxed me up and I stood at the window, letting the warmth play across my face. It felt like a benediction."

Tian looked down into her mug, as though the tea leaves held a revelation. "Thank you."

"When this madness is over," I said, "I'm going to study my own case. If I can figure out how to synthesize the herb that Alexa found, you'll be the first to know."

Before she could reply, several sets of footsteps became audible in the hall. A moment later, Malcolm emerged, Alexa and Constantine behind him. Tian's professional façade immediately snapped back into place.

"Good afternoon. Did you rest well, I hope?"

"Very well," Malcolm replied. "Thank you for the accommodations. The others will be here in a moment. They are finishing a call with Consortium Headquarters."

I rose from my chair, wanting a moment with Alexa. "How are you feeling?" I asked as I pulled her aside.

She brushed a quick kiss across my lips. "Better. Sharper." She cocked her head slightly. "What were you discussing?"

"Sunlight." I smoothed my thumb along her jaw, then stepped back as Summers and Foster rounded the corner. "I'll tell you all about it later. Looks like it's time to figure out the game plan."

❖

The house hummed with activity. It was nearly six o'clock, just shy of sunset. Soon we would be on the move again in four separate vehicles—one decoy, one scout, and two comprising the caravan that would head for the airfield where the Consortium jet would be waiting to take us all back to New York. Alexa, Karma, and I would scout ahead in the Jeep, while several of Tian's entourage would use the Humvee as the decoy.

I adjusted my gun belt, zipped up my vest, and turned to Alexa. "I'm ready."

She glanced at Karma, who was riffling through her duffle bag, and grabbed my hand. "I'm not," she murmured and led me into the hall.

The bathroom was unoccupied and she pulled me inside, then locked the door. Pressing her back to the wall, she twined her arms around my neck.

"God only knows what we'll find out there, or what will find us. You need to be strong. Drink, Valentine."

The food prepared earlier by Tian's servants had satisfied my hunger but not my thirst. I stared into Alexa's eyes, emerald pools shining with love and promising peace, and let myself surrender to my own need. Blazing a trail of kisses from her collarbone to her earlobe, I forced myself to claim her tenderly, telegraphing the magnitude of my emotion even as my teeth parted her skin. She gasped, clutching me harder as I drew from her vein. Her desire was headier than the finest perfume, and I cursed our imminent departure when her body called mine with such strength.

As I eased my teeth from her, I licked the small wounds until they closed beneath my tongue. Her fingers played in the short hairs at the back of my neck as she worked to steady her breaths.

I kissed her softly. "I promise we'll do that properly next time."

"We'd better." She caressed my face, then reached for the doorknob. "I need you."

Karma joined us in the hall, and as we made our way downstairs, I exulted in the clarity of the world around me, rendered bright and crisp by Alexa's gift of blood. Every thought, every movement became more precise, and I embraced the strength and vitality flowing through me.

Summers flagged me down on our way through the kitchen. "We have people doing flyovers of the area. They'll be in touch about any suspicious activity."

"Sounds good." I looped my Bluetooth headset over one ear as we exited into the garage. Almost everyone was gathered there already. When Constantine saw us, he approached.

"We just got the green light. The Jeep is out front. Tian's caravan will be ten minutes behind you."

Alexa embraced him quickly. "Be safe."

"And you."

We departed without fanfare. I settled in behind the wheel, Alexa beside me, while Karma took the backseat. The airfield was located to the north and west of our location, outside the city limits. The first fifteen miles passed uneventfully as we followed the route Malcolm and Tian had agreed upon. Occasionally, it doubled back on itself, allowing us to determine whether we were being followed.

Traffic grew sparser as we distanced ourselves from the city, but as the scenery became more rural so did the chances of being beset upon by Brenner's soldiers.

Shortly after we merged onto the country road that would lead us directly to the airfield, my cell phone rang.

"Missionary, this is Spotter One," came a male voice. "A small force is lying in wait two miles ahead. We suspect an ambush. Detour as soon as possible."

I slowed the car. "Ambush ahead," I reported to Karma and Alexa. "Any suggestions?"

Alexa consulted the GPS. "This is the only road. You could turn around, skirt the city, and make an approach from the north, but they'd probably have that side covered, too."

"What about off-road? Is that an option?"

"There's a lake between us and the airfield," she said. "But—"

"It might be frozen," I finished. "Spotter One, tell me about the status of the lake to the…"

"Northeast."

"Northeast. Think I could drive across it?"

While the surveillance team checked into that idea, I pulled off the road and cut the engine, not wanting to betray our position in case Brenner also had people in the air.

"I'll call Malcolm," Karma said.

"Missionary, we're seeing ice-fishing huts and a few ATVs along the edge of the lake," the spotter reported a few minutes later. "Nothing out in the middle, but our best guess—taking into account depth charts and local temperature gradients available online—is that it should be frozen solid."

"Roger." I glanced back at Karma, who gave me the thumbs-up. We had Malcolm's approval. "That's where we're headed. Stay in touch."

I hung up, started the car, and flipped on the high beams. I leaned over and kissed Alexa, hard. And then I gunned the engine.

The first few minutes were the worst, as we descended into the shallow basin where the lake lay. Pitched and jostled by the bumpy ride, I worked to maintain both the Jeep's balance and its momentum. Finally, the ride smoothed out as we approached the shoreline. Small huts dotted the coast closer to the road, but the path before us was clear.

"Our orders are to cross the lake, then wait in concealment on the far side in case we're needed," Karma reported from her ongoing conversation with Malcolm. "Now that the game's up, our decoy vehicle is being rerouted to assist us if necessary."

"Take it slow," Alexa said. "If you drive too quickly, you could create waves under the ice."

"I'm glad you grew up in Wisconsin," I said as I nosed the Jeep onto the lake. I had expected a thick layer of snow to be coating the surface, but gusting winds must have worked to partially clear the ice. Breathing shallowly, I listened with all my might for the sound of a crack.

After what felt like an eternity, we reached the far shore and I backed the Jeep into a copse of trees so we had a clear view of the caravan's approach. Alexa reached for my hand and I allowed myself to relax ever so slightly.

"That wasn't so bad," I murmured. "Thanks for the advice."

"The caravan is just leaving the road," said Karma, still on the phone with Malcolm.

My cell rang again. "Missionary, this is Spotter One." The voice was breathless, his words clipped. "The ambush force has mobilized. They have ascertained Tian's destination and are on an intercept course, due east of your present location."

"Good work," I said, forcing my voice to remain calm. "If you can give us any help from up there, now's the time." I cut the call and fired up the engine. "The ambush force has figured us out. They're trying to cut off the caravan. Tell Malcolm we're going to trip them up if we can."

When Karma relayed the message, I could hear the chaos through her receiver. Adrenaline raced through my blood as I steered back onto the icy surface. This time I pushed a little faster, knowing that Brenner would not be cautious. Just shy of the middle of the lake, I parked the car with the passenger side facing east.

"Hand me my sniper rifle please, Karma. And, babe, how do you feel about driving?"

I would have only a few seconds before their own shooters would be able to retaliate, but in those seconds I could at least do some damage. Alexa and I swapped places, and as I inspected my weapon I heard them readying their shotguns.

"Once they're on to us, I'm going to drive toward them on an angle." Alexa turned to face me. "Will you keep shooting while we're in motion?"

I nodded. "And when we're in shotgun range, Karma can join in, too."

As I powered down the window, the freezing night air sluiced into the car. I set the rifle on the sill and peered through my infrared scope. I would aim for tires first and then for the drivers, in the hopes of incapacitating at least one of their vehicles.

"Here they come," I said as several heat signatures descended from the bank. "Four of them."

Releasing a deep breath, I emptied my mind, took aim, and squeezed the trigger. My fourth shot hit the lead car's tire, causing it to veer wildly to the left. My sixth shot hit the driver of the third vehicle.

Suddenly, Alexa gasped and the world exploded. Shockwaves skipped us like pebbles across the surface, and it was a miracle that our Jeep didn't roll. On the north edge of the lake, a ball of fire roared toward the heavens.

"It fell," she said. "I saw it falling in the rearview mirror. Is it our spotter plane?"

Karma was shouting into the phone. Brenner's vehicles had also been scattered by the impact, but already, they were reforming their ranks. The caravan had been far enough away not to suffer a debilitating disruption from the blast and was approaching the center of the lake.

Alexa turned the wheel and stepped on the accelerator, but the Jeep didn't move. "Damn it! Are we stuck?"

I heard a loud cracking sound at the same time that Karma pointed out her window. "What is *that*?"

It swooped down like a bird of prey, silent and menacing—a helicopter, but somehow silent, soldiers clinging to its landing skids. They took out the tires of both caravan vehicles with surgical precision, causing each to tip onto its side, easy pickings for Brenner's approaching squad.

"Forget the car," I shouted. "Let's get over there on foot and help!"

I shoved open my door, stepped onto the frozen surface, and immediately broke into a run. Only moments later, I was thrown off my feet as a second tremor rocked the lake. After skidding painfully along the jagged ice, I finally regained my footing. When I glanced over at where the plane had crashed, all I could see was a column of fire reaching toward the heavens.

Alexa had remained on her feet and I raced after her, focusing on the shadowy figures that swarmed over the disabled caravan. Gunshots snapped the air as our team scrambled to defend Tian against Brenner's attack. When flames began to lick at the underbelly of one of the vehicles, I pushed myself even faster. One of the bullets must have pierced the gas tank.

Over the gunfire, a woman screamed. As the blaze rose higher, I shielded my eyes against the eerie light, trying to pinpoint Brenner's soldiers. Several people leapt out of one window, but I couldn't tell who they were. Without any idea of who was inside those vehicles, or whether Brenner had succeeded in capturing Tian, I couldn't risk firing at anyone. We needed to get in the mix as soon as possible, but the flames, fanned by the wind from the chopper's rotors, had become a blazing wall. As I began to skirt the wreckage, the fire crackled in my ears, drowning out whatever Alexa was trying to shout to me.

And then a splitting crack rent the air as my world tilted sideways. Fractured by the explosion, weakened by the burning caravan, the ice beneath us gave way. The water's chill was an icy hand squeezing my heart, my lungs, and I struggled not to panic. Swim up—I had to swim up. But when I tried to move my legs, they felt as though they'd been tied to an anchor. Sluggishly, I pushed through the water, trying to lift myself to the surface. Every stroke, every kick, was a battle against the extra weight of my heavy clothes and weapons. Even as the chill pierced every cell of my body, my lungs began to burn in protest. The surface. Which way was the surface?

When my right hand brushed soft fur, I realized Karma and Alexa must have shifted. Surely, their beasts knew the way to the surface. Pumping my frozen legs, I struggled to move in their direction as the dark water churned all around me.

Finally, my head broke the surface. I sucked in a breath and choked on the smoke that wreathed the gap where the vehicles had been. The collapse had sucked them both under. I could dimly hear the chopper's whirring rotors, but it sounded as though it was on the move. It had returned to stealth mode—no lights appeared in the sky, and the only illumination came from the ball of fire to the north.

The chopper's departure must have stirred the frigid water, because a wave broke over my head, filling my mouth and seeping into my lungs. Coughing, I used every ounce of my superhuman strength in my fight to remain above water. Through watering eyes, I saw Alexa crouching on the edge of the ice, panting heavily. When I reached the ledge, I pumped my legs with all my might, scrabbling for purchase as I forced my body upward. Once my elbows were braced, I kicked and pulled until I finally rolled onto the ice and lay still, gasping for air.

Alexa limped toward me and butted her head against my legs. I knew what she was trying to tell me. The edge wasn't safe, and I had to move. After failing to push myself onto my knees, I army-crawled over the jagged surface. Frigid water streamed into my eyes and every breath felt like fire. My teeth were chattering so strongly that I couldn't have spoken even if I'd wanted to. *Keep moving.* I clung to the thought as though it were a lifeline.

Only when Alexa whined deep in her throat did I stop. Between the darkness and my blurred vision, it was nearly impossible to see her, but I knew she was trying to communicate something to me. She turned away from the shore and took a few halting steps before looking back to see if I would follow. Where was she going? We needed to get back to land, not stay in the middle of the lake. When

I didn't immediately move, her lips curled and a growl welled up from deep in her throat. Clearly, she knew or could sense something that I didn't. I had to trust her.

My muscles wanted to remain immobile, but to stop moving was to give in to hypothermia. As I crawled after her, I tried to protect my frozen hands by pulling the heavy, waterlogged sleeves of my jacket down over my palms.

"Alexa?"

The faint, shivering voice belonged to Foster, and I finally understood why Alexa had steered us in this direction. Moments later, we found her sprawled on the ice, clutching her left ankle.

"Where's Karma?" I forced the words through my chattering teeth. "Are you injured?"

"Twisted my ankle getting out," she stammered. "Think Karma's trying to find the others."

As she spoke, I forced my numb fingers to pry at the straps of my weapons until they no longer clung to my back, and then I clawed at the zippers on my vest. One of the pockets held a flare. Our decoy vehicle was still out there somewhere, and if I could light the flare I might be able to guide them to our location. Then again, I risked another attack if Brenner's chopper was still in the vicinity.

Once I found the flare, I held it up to show the others. "Know it's risky. But we need help."

"Do it," Foster rasped.

When Alexa dipped her head in assent, I fumbled with the protective cap and finally managed to ignite the flare. Struggling to my knees over the protests of my burning nerves, I held it out away from my body and waved it through the air.

Suddenly, every muscle in Alexa's body tightened as she sniffed the air. Futilely, I lowered my aching arm. If an enemy was nearby, the damage had already been done. But instead of growling into the night, she began to purr. Within seconds, Constantine, Karma, and Malcolm slipped out of the shadows and into the red ring of light created by the flare. Water dripped from their fur, and blood leaked slowly from a long gash across Malcolm's flank. But they were alive.

"Thank god," I muttered.

"Leon?" asked Foster. When Constantine shook his sleek head, her face fell. "Damn."

As one, the Weres snapped to attention and turned toward the far shore. Moments later, I heard the low rumble of an engine. Praying that it was our decoy and not some remnant of Brenner's offensive, I continued to hold the flare aloft.

The Weres retreated into the shadows as the vehicle approached, and I fumbled for my pistol. Even if it was waterlogged, I could still use it as a hand weapon. But when the Humvee flashed its headlights and pulled up next to us, my anxiety eased.

Jonah jumped down from the car and raced toward us. "What happened?"

"He got her," I said, tasting the bitterness in my own words.

Jonah's mouth set into a hard line. "Where?"

Foster pointed skyward. "Chopper. Stealthed. Shot down our spotter plane."

"But we had two planes up, didn't we?" When Malcolm's rumbling growl confirmed my suspicions, I gestured toward Jonah. "Help me up and get me the second plane on audio."

With one of my arms around his shoulders, I managed to stumble to the side of the car, where he clamped a set of headphones around my ears. Sucking in a deep breath, I willed my teeth to stop chattering.

"Spotter Two, This is Valentine Darrow. Are you still in the air?"

"Yes, Missionary, and bearing toward your position."

"Negative. Brenner and his men have captured Tian and are escaping in a helicopter using stealth technology. Go after them, and in the meantime, inform Headquarters. They might be able to help track him. He is our number one priority."

"Understood, ma'am."

When I turned back, the shifters were gone. "Where—"

"To hunt," grunted Foster, who was in the process of being helped toward the back of the vehicle by two of Tian's retinue. "They'll meet us on shore."

Jonah provided us with blankets, and I stripped down to my underwear before wrapping one around me. The wool scratched my skin, but its warmth and dryness was such a relief that I didn't mind. By the time the car had reached dry land, all four Weres were waiting. Alexa was the first to pile into the back of the Humvee, and I reached behind the seats to stroke her ears as the odor of wet fur filled the car.

"Stay four-legged for now, baby. Foster and I used all the blankets."

"Your orders, Missionary?" Jonah asked as he put the car into gear.

"Drive to the airfield. Someone get through to the pilot and tell him to warm up the jet. I want us in the air the second we're on board."

Twenty minutes later, I forced my aching legs up the stairway and into the belly of the plane. Tian's servants had elected to return to the safe house and await orders from their second-in-command while we continued our pursuit. Foster and I threw ourselves into the first row of seats and strapped in, the shifters crowding around our feet for takeoff. For one surreal moment, I felt like I was in a remake of *The Swiss Family Robinson*.

Once the jet was airborne, the shifters returned to human form. After raiding the closet, we convened in the conference room. I found the first aid kit for Foster as Malcolm patched through to Headquarters. As I slid into the seat next to Alexa, I reached for her hand and laced our fingers together.

"Doing okay? Or whatever passes for that these days?"

She rested her head on my shoulder briefly. "Pardon my French, but what a clusterfuck. I'm just glad we made it through."

"You're certain?" Malcolm's terse voice echoed in the small space. "Do we have any aircraft in that region that can be scrambled? Very well."

He raised the microphone on his headset away from his mouth and turned to face us. "The spotter plane lost Brenner almost immediately, but our people at NORAD's post in Winnipeg believe they may have picked him up. He appears to be moving up the coast, toward Alaska."

"Do we have a base of operations there?" Constantine asked.

"Fairbanks," Karma chimed in as Malcolm continued to listen to the report from Headquarters. "A safe house with a command center and bomb shelter in the basement."

Pushing my fatigue aside, I got to my feet. "I'll tell the pilot. Fairbanks, here we come."

CHAPTER THIRTEEN

The Consortium's safe house in Fairbanks was in fact a private estate east of the city, set on a hundred acres of forested land. As we traveled there by Land Rover, Karma told us that the Consortium had a strong presence in the area. The Alaskan wilderness, with its wide-open spaces and long wintry nights, was friendly both to wereshifters and vampires at this time of year. A skeleton crew remained at the estate year-round to monitor activity and handle emergencies, and they would be able to help us in our mission.

Our people at NORAD had lost track of Brenner's aircraft just after it crossed the Alaskan state line, so we were still searching for a needle in a haystack. Despite the odds, Malcolm was more energized than I had ever seen him. During our discussion on the jet, he had theorized that Brenner was taking Tian to some sort of base or installation. If we could manage to pinpoint its location and organize an offensive, we could take out not only Brenner, but also his seat of operations.

The dawn was still hours away when the car paused at the guardhouse just outside a tall, wrought iron gate. A fence of the same height, topped with several feet of barbed wire, extended both to the left and right as far as I could see. Once our identities had been verified, the guard waved us through and we proceeded down a long, winding driveway. After several minutes, the lane opened into a circular space illuminated by floodlights. Directly ahead, a large stone house, complete with two turrets, towered into the night. A matching outbuilding, set fifty yards to the left, appeared to be a garage.

Outside the front door stood a tall African-American woman dressed in battle fatigues, her dark hair pulled back in a tight bun. When we emerged from the car, she greeted Malcolm by his title and introduced herself as Natasha Berbridge. I raised one eyebrow at Alexa.

"Shifter," she murmured under her breath. "A bear."

"We are at your disposal," Natasha said once Malcolm had made introductions. "There are more than enough bedrooms on the second floor to accommodate your needs."

"Take a few moments to situate yourselves," Malcolm said. "We'll reconvene in the command center in a quarter-hour."

The foyer was tall, its walls bare and imposing. To the right, I caught a glimpse of a spacious kitchen, stainless steel appliances gleaming. The staircase rose immediately before us, and I let Alexa precede me. She turned left at the top and ducked into the first bedroom. As soon as I closed the door behind us, she was in my arms, face buried in the crook of my neck. I stroked her back and inhaled deeply, taking comfort in the sweetness of her scent.

Finally, she pulled back just enough to look into my eyes. "Is there any chance that tomorrow will be a day when we don't have a near-death experience?"

I managed to crack a smile. "It's tomorrow already, remember? And somehow, I doubt it. But at least we can meet whatever's coming together."

"What do you think he's going to do to Tian, Val? Will he kill her once he gets what he needs?"

Hoping to comfort us both, I continued to rub slow circles on her lower back. "I don't think so. At least, not at first. He'll need to keep her alive until he's figured out a way to manufacture the parasite."

"To weaponize it."

I nodded, and for a long moment we stood still, simply looking at each other. And then, quite suddenly, her hands were in my hair and her body was flush against mine as she crushed our lips together in a fiercely passionate kiss. My thirst flared as our tongues tangled, and I dug my fingertips into the ridges of muscle above her hips, clutching her tightly. As I pushed her against the wall, she reached for my right hand and shoved it beneath the waistband of her pants.

Finding her hot and slick, I scissored my fingers against her and kissed my way down to her neck. As I teased her pulse point with my tongue, she pressed my head closer.

"Inside," she gasped.

I filled her with my fingers and slipped my teeth into her vein, thrilling to the guttural moan that greeted my entry. The sunburst of her blood cascaded into my empty stomach as I slid slowly in and out of her body, stoking her pleasure. When I brought my thumb down firmly against her, she shuddered in my arms, and I groaned against her skin at the sensation of her inner walls clenching around me.

When the aftershocks passed, I gently withdrew from her body. As I caught the last drops of her glorious blood on my tongue, she stroked the nape of my neck.

"I hate that we don't have time for me to touch you."

I smiled against her skin. "I know. But you give me so much, baby. I love you."

She pulled my head up. "Once this is all over, I want to go away. Just the two of us. Back to that cabin in the Catskills."

"That sounds wonderf—"

A knock at the door interrupted us, and I reluctantly pulled away to answer it. Karma stood on the other side, and I could tell immediately that she'd heard some sort of news. Her jackal was close to the surface, and energy crackled around her.

"There's been a development."

We hurried into the basement, where Malcolm, Natasha, and Constantine were already seated at an oval conference table. A sliding glass door separated the conference room from a small chamber that resembled Hollywood's portrayal of Mission Control, with several computer banks facing a large screen. I caught sight of Foster inside, hunched over one of the monitors. She was probably communicating with Helen, and I wondered what sort of political maneuverings were happening amongst the Sunrunners at this very moment, now that Tian was in Brenner's custody.

Malcolm didn't waste a second. "Brenner just issued another ultimatum."

My pulse spiked. Brenner's last ultimatum had nearly sent Helen to her death, and the one before that had nearly started a war between wereshifters and vampires. Alexa sat down, but I remained standing, palms flat on the table.

"Brenner has declared his intention to release a biological weapon that will destroy all vampires. He hasn't been any more specific than that."

"What does he want?" Alexa asked.

"Surrender. Of the entire species. Every vampire who turns him or herself in will, he alleges, be spared."

"Spared. Right." I shook my head. "He'll either kill us on the spot or throw us into concentration camps."

"Agreed," Malcolm said. "Helen has already disseminated her own message, urging no one to believe his offer to be merciful."

"Do we have any new intel on his possible position?" Karma asked.

"We've diverted all available surveillance resources to inspecting data from satellites and recent flyovers," said Constantine. "Hopefully, we'll have a lead soon."

"In the meantime, take this opportunity to rest," said Malcolm. "If we receive any promising intelligence, you will be needed to investigate."

Alexa rose and grabbed my hand, tugging as she moved toward the stairs. I paused on the bottom step and gestured toward the computer banks.

"I should check in with Bridget. And with Olivia."

Her eyes narrowed. "Half an hour, tops. Then we need to sleep."

"Babe, you should just go to bed now and I'll—"

"No. I'm staying with you." Alexa reversed course but never let go of my hand. "We're sticking together. Don't argue."

Even with cheeks pale from exhaustion and dark shadows beneath her eyes, she was so beautiful. I didn't want to be parted from her either, not even by only two stories. Wisely, I didn't open my mouth—just squeezed her hand and followed her lead.

❖

A sharp rap at the door woke me from a deep sleep. Alexa sat up next to me, but when she started to swing her legs over the side of the bed, I stopped her and went myself.

"Who is it?"

"Constantine. We need you downstairs."

"We'll be there right away."

As I pulled on my clothes, I glanced at my watch. Almost two o'clock in the afternoon. Thankfully, our six hours of sleep had blunted the edge of my fatigue. My eyes no longer felt like sandpaper, and my mind was clear and sharp.

"How are you feeling?" I asked Alexa as we left the room.

"Better. Though I could have slept twice as long."

We found the conference room in much the same condition as we'd left it, except that now there were papers and photographs strewn all across the table. Constantine and Malcolm were conferring quietly at one end, and they looked up as we entered.

"We received a tip about an hour ago," Constantine said. "And it seems promising. Last night, a Canadian military plane on a flyover picked up the signature of what might be Brenner's chopper, landing at an airfield approximately one hour's drive from this location."

"Could that be the site of his base?" Alexa asked.

"It's possible," said Constantine. "We obviously haven't had the chance to do a deep analysis of the surrounding area."

"This is a thin lead," Malcolm said. "We can't attempt any kind of full assault until we get reinforcements. I sent out a mustering call to Headquarters yesterday, but you all know that we have no standing army. It will take many days for our people to gather. In the meanwhile, I want to send out a reconnaissance party now. Karma will lead the mission." He looked first to Alexa and then to me. "Can I count on you both to accompany her?"

"Of course," Alexa said.

"The object of this mission will be to determine whether this airfield is linked to Brenner, and whether you can discover any additional information about a potential base in the region."

"Where can we find the equipment we'll need?" I asked.

"Natasha will direct us to the armory," Constantine said. "I'll be coming with you as well."

Natasha led us through the computer room and into a narrow corridor that ended in a T. To the left, a staircase led up to the first floor of the house. When she turned down the short passage to their right and unlocked the small door at its end, I couldn't help but be impressed.

Three neatly organized rows of firearms stretched all the way to the back of the long, narrow chamber. The shelves that lined the walls were filled with equipment of all sorts: camouflage clothing, flak jackets, boots, canteens, night vision goggles, even satellite phones. As we moved among the inventory, I debated what kind of camo to use.

"What time is sunset? Anyone know?"

"Shortly before five o'clock," said Natasha.

I checked my watch again. "The earliest we'll make it there is four o'clock. Let's dress in blacks."

"Good plan," Constantine said as he began to riffle through the clothing. "And I'm driving."

❖

Alexa and I took turns catnapping in the backseat of the Jeep, while the others remained awake and attentive in case of trouble. While no one expected Brenner to be searching for us now that he'd captured his quarry, we couldn't afford any more setbacks. The journey passed quietly as each of us gathered strength for whatever awaited us. I couldn't stop thinking about Tian and what Brenner might have planned for her once he'd taken what he needed from her blood. And did he already have a weaponizing mechanism? A bomb, perhaps? Or a way to infect water or air supplies?

As I considered the possibilities, I found myself thinking about the problem not only as a potential victim and as a high-ranking member of the Consortium, but also as a scientist. Biology had been my first academic love. Until several months ago, I had been enrolled in medical school, committed to learning the skills I would need in order to study every aspect of the vampire parasite. Transitioning to a full vampire had altered not only my circulatory system, but also my priorities. For my entire adult life, I had tried to distance myself from my biological family, but the past few months had taught me that I had inherited my father's skill in the world of high finance.

Now that Alexa had brought me back, I needed to figure out where I wanted to focus my time and attention—if, of course, we managed to survive this latest crisis. She was napping with her head in my lap, and I dared to run my fingers through the dark hair that matched the color of her panther's fur.

When Karma instructed Constantine to pull off the road in five miles, I leaned forward to look at the topographical map she had pulled up on her tablet. She pointed to a spot where the contour lines nearly converged.

"That looks like some kind of cliff," she said. "We'll leave the Jeep in whatever cover we can find and cross the remaining two miles on foot."

Alexa had woken at the sound of our discussion and she sat up, blinking the sleep from her eyes. When I squeezed her hand, she returned the pressure briefly before beginning to double-check her gear. She handed me a pair of night vision goggles and I settled them over the cap of my black knit ski mask.

Constantine pulled off the road where Karma indicated, and I braced myself against the frame of the car as the snow tires lumbered across the ice and snow. Almost immediately, the land began to slope up, and he carefully maneuvered the Jeep into a small space between a large boulder and the rising ridge.

Dry, icy air pierced my lungs as I opened the door, and I quickly pulled the ski mask down to cover my face. After collecting our weapons, we huddled around Karma and the map.

"Once we're over the ridge, fan out in increments of fifty yards. We'll converge on this point here, which is the hangar." She tapped her ear bud. "No transmitting unless it's an emergency."

I flipped the goggles down over my eyes and fell into line behind Alexa as we began our ascent. Packed snow crunched beneath our feet as we climbed. The slope was steep, and within minutes I no longer felt the chill in the air. Clouds scudded across the sky, mostly obscuring the light cast by the half moon.

At the top, we found ourselves standing on what appeared to be a broad plateau. I took up a flanking position to the right and focused on dividing my attention between my surroundings and the ground itself. If Brenner's chopper had landed here, either he had some sort of base underground, or he had travelled elsewhere. Either way, the landscape might betray secrets.

But as time passed, I saw no sign of any recent human activity. The only tracks I encountered belonged to animals, and none of the paw prints were large enough to be those of a wolf. After checking my GPS, I began angling my path more sharply toward the location of the hangar.

The airfield was surrounded by a tall chain fence. I took off one glove and touched a single finger to the metal. When no current jolted through my body, I grabbed hold and began to scale it. The fact that it wasn't electric didn't mean it wasn't somehow alarmed, but that was a risk we'd have to take. After several minutes spent crossing tundra, I reached a runway. It had been paved recently— the asphalt was laced with very few cracks—but I found no sign of tire tracks. No airplanes had landed since the last snowfall. Perhaps our analysts would discover activity if they looked at the satellite footage from earlier in the month.

As I moved closer to the hangar, I concentrated on moving silently over the crusty snow. My feet didn't hit asphalt again until I reached a large paved lot leading up to the hangar that loomed, dark and hulking, a hundred yards away. Several large vehicles were parked near the entrance, but my goggles had yet to pick up on any signs of life.

Out of the corner of my eyes, I caught a flicker of motion—Alexa, also converging onto the building. I moved close to her as we converged on the nearest side of the building

"Constantine and Karma went around the far side," she whispered.

I nodded. Ahead of us, the amorphous vehicles had resolved into two snowcats and a pickup truck. Wanting no surprises, I pulled out the Glock I'd commandeered from the outpost and leapt lightly into the bed of the truck. No one there, no one in the cab. Alexa shook her head as she peered into the first snowcat, and together, we checked the second.

When I gestured toward the right, she nodded and took the lead as we headed around the edge of the building. This was the main entrance of the hangar, and its wide, open mouth had been sealed by a metal portcullis. Constantine and Karma met us at the far corner.

"We passed a ladder to the roof," Karma said, already in motion.

She climbed up first, and I spotted her as she secured a rope to the ledge. The steeply sloping roof had been swept mostly bare by gravity and the wind, though a few stubborn patches of snow and ice clung to the flimsy surface. Clutching the rope in her hands, Karma stepped lightly across the flimsy surface.

"Skylight here," she murmured, and I relayed the message to the rest of the group.

I tossed her my own rope, which she secured to a nearby air duct and then handed back to me. She pulled out her side arm and aimed it at the square of glass, then squeezed off two rounds in quick succession. I felt Alexa take hold around my knees from below.

"Got me?"

"Always."

Muscles straining, I belayed Karma down as quickly as I could. Once the rope went slack, I followed her. The interior was pitch-dark, but her body was illuminated by my goggles. She was crouched on the floor, and I rested one hand between her shoulders.

"You okay?"

"Fine. Trying to pick up a sound or scent."

"Anything?"

She shook her head. Once the others had joined us, we fanned out and moved slowly through the hangar. I counted several shapes that looked like light aircraft in addition to two helicopters. Cabinets and shelves lined the walls, presumably filled with tools for repair. As I moved toward the back of the facility where a small space had been cordoned off for some kind of office space, I felt my skin prickle. This didn't make any sense. Why would Brenner leave such a valuable asset unguarded?

And then the world turned white as someone, somewhere, turned on the lights.

Ripping off my goggles, I threw myself to the ground and began to roll, ears ringing from the burst of gunfire coming from somewhere ahead of me. Was this an ambush? Or had the guard of the installation somehow been alerted to our presence when we crossed the perimeter?

The scent of blood filled the air and saliva flooded my mouth. Behind me, I heard a groan followed by the sounds of snarling as someone shifted. Praying Alexa hadn't been hit, I pushed hard off the floor and landed in a low crouch. A man stood in the doorway of the office, a machine gun raised to his shoulder. Even as I watched, its barrel swung toward where Karma was partially concealed behind the wing of a biplane. Before I could reach for my weapon, he fired and hit her in the legs. As she dropped to the ground, the air around her began to shimmer.

In an instant, my Glock was in hand. But as I raised it and aimed at our attacker, I heard a small, plinking sound behind me, like a screw rolling across the floor. I ducked and spun, only to find nothing but empty air. Cursing beneath my breath, I turned back to the shooter and fired twice quickly, hoping at least to distract him enough for Karma to gain the advantage.

But before I could tell whether either of my bullets had flown true, a heavy blow struck the side of my head. Pain blazed through my skull and I staggered to the side, crashing into the wall. Moments later, a spear of agony lanced through my calf and I crumpled to the floor. Ears ringing, vision blurred, I caught a flash of motion to my left and squeezed the trigger again. A low grunt, followed by a string of what sounded like curses in a language I couldn't understand, gave me hope that I'd found my mark. And then pain shot through my chest as someone's foot connected with my rib cage, over and over and over until every tortured gasp for air sent spikes of agony radiating throughout my torso.

Someone grabbed the back of my jacket and hauled me across the floor. Over the ringing in my ears I heard a loud grinding sound from above and then the whirr of rotor blades displacing air. My left leg burned as I was dragged up some kind of ramp and then dumped onto a metal floor. When I tried to take stock of my surroundings, my blurred vision sent nausea spiraling through my gut. Was I in the chopper? Where were they taking me? Why hadn't they simply killed me? And where was Alexa? Was she safe?

The sensation of rising. Ears popping. Low, guttural voices speaking…what? Some kind of Eastern European language, maybe? The pain lashed at my body like a riptide, pulling me under only to toss me back onto the jagged shore of consciousness. Bloodied and broken, curled into a ball with my injured leg awkwardly outstretched, I could retain no sense of time. Whether minutes or hours had passed before we began to descend, I couldn't tell.

When the chopper finally touched down, its landing jarred me and a groan escaped before I could seal my lips against it. Again, I was seized and dragged along the ground. Every inch forward was a world of agony, and I clenched my teeth to stop myself from betraying any weakness.

Only when my captors halted did I dare to open my eyes. I was lying on my back on some kind of gravel surface, out under the night sky. Hulking shadowy figures stood in a ring around me, but I was unable to focus on their faces.

All I could think was that I didn't want to die like this. I would not let them have the satisfaction of defeat. I would not quit. I would not lie down. Fighting through the pain and nausea, I pushed myself up on one knee, determined to fight. The dark forms above me laughed.

Their ranks parted, and a man stepped into the middle of the circle to loom over me. I couldn't see his eyes, but his smile was cruel, and in one hand he held a gun.

"I've waited a long time to make your acquaintance, Valentine," he said.

A flash of pain struck my temple, streaking across my battered consciousness like a deadly comet. And then my world went dark.

CHAPTER FOURTEEN

My head reverberated with sound, light, and heat. Through the painful din, I struggled to latch on to something, anything that would anchor me in the maelstrom. Flames. I remembered flames—the fire from the spotter plane's crash along the lakeshore. The freezing water. Gunfire in the hangar. A spear of agony in my leg. The cruel face looming above me.

I was alive. Badly injured, but alive.

When I opened my eyes, the light pierced into my brain like nails and the room spun in a blur, driving bile up into my mouth. Slamming my eyelids shut, I swallowed quickly and focused on taking slow, rhythmic breaths until the nausea subsided. Wherever Brenner was keeping me, the air had a stale and antiseptic taste to it that reminded me of every hospital I'd been in. But I couldn't rely solely on my sense of smell to gather enough information for me to figure out how to escape. Taking another few deep breaths, I opened my eyes to take in the barest sliver of my scenery.

Whiteness was all that greeted me, as though I'd been plunged into some kind of evanescent fog. Carefully, I opened my eyes even further, but either my vision was blurred or the room actually was shrouded in a deep mist. My stomach roiled and I counted to twenty before attempting anything more. After what felt like hours, I had finally regained a full field of vision, but the world was still blurry— due, I was sure, to the head trauma I'd endured from Brenner and his men.

I tried to sit up and choked violently as something hard and cold struck my windpipe. It felt like a band of metal, and it was suspended inches above my neck. Coughing made the roaring heat in my head echo louder, and I struggled to regain my steady breathing. I was a captive. That was the only certainty. I had to be patient and learn what Brenner had done to me—to think through the pain so I could escape and return to Alexa.

The white ceiling was broken only by an oval fluorescent lamp. With excruciating slowness, I moved my head as far as I could—only an inch either way—and shifted my eyes to each side. Whiteness everywhere. I flexed my fingers, then my toes. Beneath the dull pounding in my brain, I felt each digit. No damage to my spine, then. Like my neck, my limbs were held to the table by unyielding bands. My arms were stretched perpendicular to my body, and my thighs had been spread wide. I was naked, vulnerable, and open. My wounded leg throbbed, and renewed nausea churned in my stomach as I wondered whether I would feel other kinds of pain when the headache finally subsided.

Panic welled up to fill the ache in my chest, but as my heart began to race, the pressure in my head grew even worse. I had to remain calm, or I would be of no use to anyone. To distract myself, I exercised my intellect. Brenner needed Tian to complete that infernal experiment on the parasite, but what did he want with me? He had tried to assassinate me on three separate occasions, but if he wanted me dead, why hadn't he ordered his soldiers to kill me on sight? They'd had plenty of chances, and so had he.

But the longer I lay there, bound and helpless, the more my logical brain struggled to keep the panic at bay. Thirst burned in my throat, and though I knew that was my body's natural reaction to being injured, it only increased my sense of claustrophobia. Did Brenner plan to keep me here, bound and helpless, until my appetite drove me insane? Would he gloat over me as I slowly starved to death? Or worse—what if, when my sanity had fled, he offered me a human victim? Would I be able to keep my promise to Alexa and resist the needs of the parasite?

Deep down, I knew that in such a desperate case, she would feel only sympathy and compassion. She would want me to feed. I could practically hear her voice soothing me, telling me that we would be all right. Reminding me that she had brought me back once and could do it again. But I didn't want her to have to say those things. I wanted to be stronger than my appetite, strong enough to uphold the vows I'd sworn both to her and to myself. For now, I had to find a way to sublimate my thirst—to transform it into a motivating force and not a crippling one.

But as time passed—whether in minutes or hours, I had no way of knowing—the roaring in my head was eclipsed by body-wracking shivers that jammed my windpipe against the metal ring. I coughed uncontrollably, tears running down my cheeks to plink onto the metal slab that was my prison. Had Brenner given me something to send me into these paroxysms? Or were they simply my nervous system's reaction to the trauma and stress? Flashes of heat and cold surged beneath my skin like electrical currents, and dimly I wondered whether I was becoming feverish. Within moments, a layer of sweat had coated my limbs and was trickling down onto the table. Closing my eyes, I fought to keep my muscles loose and relaxed.

Mercifully, the trembling finally subsided. The sharp waves of pain in my head refused to let me sleep, but for a while I found myself able to drift somewhere between consciousness and oblivion. And then a door opened, sending discernable eddies through the air current. The reverberation of heavy footsteps on a bare floor increased the throbbing in my head. Even as my senses strained for some clue about my visitor, I stared straight up, mouth set in a grim line. No matter who it was, I wouldn't give them the satisfaction of seeing anything resembling fear or uncertainty.

A broad finger dipped into my navel, and I barely managed to suppress a shudder. The foreign touch moved slowly up until it came to a halt between my breasts. Brenner's smiling face entered my field of vision, and my lip curled in disgust as his features swam in and out of focus.

"Valentine Darrow." His voice was jovial. "You have been such a thorn in my side. And now, look at you."

I held his gaze and my tongue, vowing to remain unbroken no matter what he did to me. When he left my field of view and began to pace the length of the room, my every muscle tensed, dreading the return of his touch.

"You've been lying here for several hours," he said conversationally, as though we were discussing the weather. "I offered you to my soldiers—both the men and the women. Not a single one of them wanted anything to do with you. How does it feel, Valentine, to be so utterly repulsive that no one will so much as *rape* you?"

I wanted to laugh in his face. Only a genocidal psychopath would consider that an insult. Abruptly, he loomed over me again, his smile even wider.

"On the other hand, I'm sure they'll have no such compunctions about your lover. When the time comes, I promise you'll have a front row seat."

I spat in his face, but he had expected it and dodged easily. Despite my vow not to show any emotion, I didn't regret what I'd done. Never, ever would I let him or his cronies touch Alexa. I would find a way to stop him, no matter the cost.

"But perhaps by then, your priorities will have changed," he continued. "Soon, you will become part of my little experiment. Once I'm done with you, you may not care about your precious Alexa at all. I really must thank you for allowing me to kill two birds with one stone, as it were."

I had no idea what he was talking about, and the question must have shown in my expression. He laughed again.

"Are you really so ignorant? Since the Consortium rushed to protect Tian, I can only assume that you're aware of the modified parasite and how it can be engineered. I stole six samples—true. But the Sunrunner variant was not the only missing piece of the puzzle."

Epiphany dawned like a bomb blast. The sample from the blood prime of the Missionary clan had been from my predecessor, René, whom Brenner had killed. It was useless. Brenner needed blood from me to complete the experiment—blood that, I was certain, he had already collected. Frustration lashed through me like a lightning storm, and I ground my sharpened teeth together.

"Once we have successfully engineered the hybrid parasite, you'll have the distinction of becoming a lab rat. Apparently, breeding this parasite in the circulatory system of a blood prime will fix it in its current form. So even if I do kill you, or that Sunrunner cunt, this specimen will continue to function." He bared his teeth in a smile. "Incidentally, Helen's notes suggest that the infection process is exquisitely painful. My words, not hers."

I could barely comprehend his gloating. My brain spun wildly, refusing to process his sinister promise. In craving the blood of vampires, I would be doomed to hunt them down until they were extinct. And then I would die of starvation.

"That expression on your face is priceless, Valentine. Pity I don't have a camera." Brenner's footsteps retreated. "In the meantime, I haven't yet decided whether I'll move you into more humane facilities, or let you piss all over yourself on this table like the vermin you are. In the meantime, enjoy contemplating your fate."

And then he was gone.

❖

Time passed. At least, that's what I told myself. The light never changed, and no sound penetrated into the room. I had no way of marking the hours, and after a while, I caught my psyche trying to play tricks on my rational mind.

Maybe you've always been here, it whispered. Maybe Alexa was only a dream. Or wishful thinking. Or a figment of your imagination. Maybe you died in the lake, or at the hands of Brenner's soldiers. Maybe this is hell, and your mother was right after all.

Once I realized that I was on the cusp of hallucination, I fought back with Descartes. I think, therefore I am. I exist. I can remember the chain of events that brought me here, and one day, I will escape.

Alexa is still alive, and I will find her. We will bring Brenner to justice and then we will live out the rest of eternity together, at peace in each other even if the world itself goes up in flames.

I had to keep my brain sharp and my psyche strong. Forcing my thoughts back in time, I sifted through my memories of Alexa, desperate to cling to every sensual detail. To anchor myself to her even as oblivion threatened from within and without.

Suddenly, the cogs of my mind caught and latched onto my memory of our second date—of the moment when I had finally been convinced that my growing fascination with her was not one-sided. She had put me through my paces on that day, but for as long as I lived, I would never forget how strong she had made me feel. Even if I lost all sanity, some part of me would remember. I had to believe it…

The Niagra was exceptionally busy on the second day of the new year. New York City was still overrun by tourists, and the unseasonably warm weather meant that everyone was out and about. The bar was packed, and all the newcomers wanted elaborate mixed drinks. My arms were in great shape, but by eleven o'clock, soreness had crept into my muscles. And the crowd showed no signs of diminishing. In a rare lull just prior to midnight, I finally managed to gulp down water and check my phone. I had one text, and when I saw the name attached, my pulse skyrocketed.

Central park, Columbus Circle entrance. Tomorrow, 10 a.m. Dress to run.

At first, I thought she might have sent the message to the wrong person, but then I realized I didn't care. Except for one brief, fairly formal thank you e-mail the day after our elaborate dinner date almost a week ago, Alexa had been silent. I had replied with an open invitation to go out in the future but had heard no response. Now, apparently, I had a date tomorrow. Whether the text had been intended for me or not.

As I jogged up the stairs leading out of the subway the next morning, I glanced at my watch. Ten minutes to spare, though I had a feeling Alexa liked to be early. Sure enough, once I made my way to the park entrance I saw her stretching out her quads near the main gate. She wore a light blue windbreaker, and she'd pulled her red hair back into a long ponytail. Black leggings clung to her muscular thighs and sculpted calves, and she effortlessly maintained her balance even as she switched legs. Quite simply, she was breathtaking.

I could tell the moment she caught sight of me, because her body went still and her eyes widened ever so slightly. In the next moment, she adopted a look of nonchalance, but that single instant gave me a burst of confidence. I'd chosen my silver Under Armour shirt because it highlighted the muscles in my arms and abs while leaving no doubt that I was a woman. Apparently, she approved.

"Good morning," I called as I approached her.

"Hi. Glad you made it."

"Wouldn't have missed this for the world." I grabbed the fence a few feet away and began stretching out my calves. "I can't believe how warm it is."

"I know. Crazy. So, how late was your night?"

"The tourists were still out in full force. Didn't make it home until three."

"And here I made you get up early."

"No place I'd rather be." I switched to stretching out my hamstrings. "Besides, I'm bad at sleeping in."

"Why is that?"

I rose slowly out of the stretch, looking up to meet her questioning gaze.

"I don't know, exactly. Guess I'm not that good at relaxing, in general. There's…there's just a lot to do."

Leaning back down, I mentally cursed myself for my vague and ineloquent answer. Now she probably thought I was some kind of hyperactive idiot who could never sit still. But then I felt her touch on my shoulder.

"I know what you mean."

Drawing myself up to my full height, I raised my arms above my head to loosen the taut muscles in my shoulders. She was looking at me thoughtfully, and I wondered if she really meant what she'd said.

The restlessness that burned at the core of me wasn't something I had discussed very much with past girlfriends. They'd thought I had it all—the last name, the access to money, the connections. I had never known how to tell them that I didn't really care about those things. That I was driven to make my own mark on the world. Was Alexa someone who might empathize? Would she be—could she be—someone in whom I'd truly be able to confide?

When color bloomed in her cheeks and she suddenly looked away, I wondered what she'd been thinking.

"Ready?" she asked, gesturing toward the open gate.

"Whenever you are."

She walked out onto the asphalt and broke into a jog. I fell into step with her, welcoming the warm air into my lungs. Had it not been for the utter bareness of the trees, this could have passed for a morning in early April.

After descending a shallow slope, our road merged with the long loop inside the park. Alexa hadn't told me how far she wanted to run, and I wasn't about to ask her. I just hoped I could keep up.

"Let me know if you need to slow down at any point," she said.

"I'll be fine." Glancing sideways, I grinned at the challenge in her eyes. "Set any pace you like."

Immediately, she sped up, and I lengthened my stride to match. As we rounded a curve and headed uphill, we found ourselves passing many of the other runners. Currently, I did most of my running on a flat treadmill, and my calves protested the incline, but I ignored them and concentrated on taking deep, even breaths. When we reached the top of the hill, I realized we were breathing in synchrony. Suddenly exhilarated, I turned my head to watch her move. Ponytail bouncing against her shoulders, arms pumping steadily at her sides, face flushed and glistening, she was the most beautiful woman I'd ever seen. And what I loved most of all was that she was allowing me to see the real "her," not just the version in a little black dress. I had invited her to dinner with the intent to impress. She had invited me on a run with the intent to show me her true colors.

Our eyes met, and I stumbled slightly. She reached for my arm, fingertips lingering even after I'd regained my balance.

"What?"

She had showed no pretense, so I didn't either. "You're beautiful."

Laughing, she pulled her hand away and picked up speed. "I think we need to go even faster."

We ran for over an hour—through the park and then down along the West Side Highway—before Alexa slowed to a walk. After we'd stretched out, she led me to a small, nondescript diner in the West Village. She claimed it served the best Oreo milkshakes, so I ordered one along with a massive breakfast burrito topped with avocados. Technically, I'd probably had a better brunch or two, but in that moment nothing could compare.

For over an hour we sat across from each other at a table next to the window. Alexa insisted on paying. She also insisted on talking politics. When I balked, she took my hand and entwined our fingers. My heart began to race far faster than it had even on the steepest climbs of our run.

"Look, Val," she said, rubbing her thumb very gently across my knuckles. "I'm not trying to make you uncomfortable or dig up dirt about your family. I don't really care about them at the moment. But I'm starting to care about you, and I want to know what you think about…this." She waved her hand in the air. "Life. New York. The country. The world."

Stuck on her soft touch and the part about her starting to care about me, I quickly mustered my wits.

"Okay. I'm sorry if I seemed defensive. I guess I'm just not used to that."

"You're not used to other people caring what you think?" She sounded incredulous. When I shrugged, her eyes narrowed. "What about past girlfriends?"

"You might find this hard to believe," I said quietly, "but it's been a long time since I pursued someone. Women tend to want me for my last name and my family's money, not for my intellect."

Alexa arched an eyebrow and squeezed my fingers. "Not this woman. Now. You're studying to become a doctor, so you must have some thoughts about the health care crisis. Let's hear them."

Eventually, we had to give up the table, but when I offered to walk her home, she agreed. She shared an apartment in SoHo with several friends, and this time I was the one to join our hands as we began to walk. We took our time navigating the spidery streets of the Village, both of us apparently unwilling to end the conversation. She was passionate and well spoken—a true believer in social justice—and I was starting to think that her political views leaned even more heavily toward the left than did mine.

"So," I said as I steered her around a sidewalk puddle, "how does someone who just identified as 'practically a democratic socialist' decide to study corporate law?"

She smiled. "Sometimes the best way to change something is from the inside, isn't it? I think I'll be better able to accomplish my goals if I have an intimate knowledge of all the gears and cogs inside the behemoth."

"You don't think you'll be tempted to turn to the Dark Side?"

"Well, probably at some point. I just have to trust that I'm strong enough." Her eyes met mine, appraising. "Is that why you didn't follow in your father's footsteps? Temptation?"

It felt like she was staring right into my soul, and I had to stop myself from looking away. Her insight made perfect sense. How did she see so much?

"Maybe. Probably. I've never thought about it that way before."

She pulled me under the awning of a flower shop and reached up to twine her arms around my neck. Her fingertips stroked my hair as she eliminated the space between our bodies, bringing her chest flush with mine. My head spun as I let my palms come to rest on her hips. She felt incredible in my arms, and it was so hard to resist the impulse to dip my head and kiss her.

"Do you know what I think, Valentine?"

"What's that?" I breathed, lost in the patterns made by the various shades of green swirling in her eyes.

"I think you're a lot stronger than you give yourself credit for."

And then she raised herself onto her toes and kissed me.

❖

As the memory faded, I opened my eyes. The contours of the ceiling were a little crisper now, and I realized that my vision was beginning to sharpen. Had my subconscious chosen that memory for a reason? Was Alexa speaking to me even now, reminding me of my inner fortitude, inspiring me from deep inside my own psyche?

Returning back into myself, I plumbed the depths of my brain. The first time we'd made love. The first meal we'd cooked together. Staying up all night watching B-rated horror movies. Studying for final exams together on the top floor of the library. Over and over and over I traced the memories with my mind, recalling the sights, the sounds, the scents. They had happened. She was real. I was real, and I would find a way to return to her.

The door opened. Rough hands squeezed my left bicep and jammed a needle into my arm. Liquid fire streamed into my vein, then spread. My heart pounded against my ribs. Flames trailed down my abdomen, into my legs. My skin was burning. Thousands of tiny pins and needles pierced every muscle, igniting my synapses. A moan escaped before I could clench my jaw to contain it. Every cell was an agony of flame, and in that moment my mother's words came back to me. *Unless you repent, Valentine, your soul will burn in flames for eternity.*

Someone was screaming. The pain grew exponentially. Blood filled my mouth.

And then finally, darkness.

❖

I woke to the foreign sensation of softness beneath my cheek. Having learned my lesson, I took stock of my surroundings before I dared even to open my eyes. The light beyond my eyelids seemed softer than it had before, though the air still smelled of metal and antiseptic. I was curled on my right side on what felt like a mattress, and I was no longer naked. Every muscle in my body ached, my left leg throbbed in time with the pulse beating in my temples, and my throat was parched.

Questions flooded into the forefront of my consciousness. Had Brenner's men injected me with the modified parasite? Was I a cannibal? How would I know? What were Brenner's plans now? Had he turned Tian as well? How was I going to find my way back to Alexa? Was she even alive?

My heart thundered in my chest, and I opened my eyes to distract myself from the panic. I lay on a narrow cot in a rectangular, windowless room. Several feet away, another cot stood unoccupied, though its blankets were mussed. I sat up slowly, wincing as my muscles protested even the tiniest movement. Someone had dressed me in a pale blue pair of scrubs. I felt like I'd been hit by a bus. How much of the soreness was due to having been strapped to a table for eons, and how much had to do with the injection I'd received, I couldn't tell.

My thirst was strong, but it didn't feel qualitatively different from what I had experienced before. Aside from the soreness, I felt remarkably normal. When would the new parasite make itself known? If I were in the presence of a vampire, would my bloodlust take over? Cradling my head in my hands, I stared at the floor and willed myself to stay calm.

"Now that you're awake, the show can begin." Brenner's disembodied voice filled the room. Before I could control myself, I had jumped to my feet, adrenaline propelling my aching body into motion. I scanned the room, head pounding, but I couldn't pinpoint the camera.

Brenner's laughter at my reaction was overshadowed by the whir of electronics as part of the far wall retracted to reveal a pane of glass looking out on an examination room. Aside from the stainless steel table that was bolted into the center of the floor, the room was empty. This place, or something like it, was surely where I had been kept. Bile rose into my throat, but I forced it back. I would not give Brenner the satisfaction of seeing me choke on my own fear.

The door to the examination room opened and a man was shoved inside. His dark hair was greasy, his clothing unkempt. He stared at his surroundings with wide, suspicious eyes. Letting his fingers trail along the wall, he traced the circumference of the room.

"My soldiers caught this piece of filth draining the blood from a teenage girl in an alleyway behind a cinema. She survived, thankfully. He won't be so fortunate."

Again, the door opened. This time I recognized the person who staggered inside. Tian. She looked to be on the edge of sanity; sweat dampened her hairline and her fingertips were ragged and bleeding. Red furrows marred her arms below sleeves identical to mine. She had been self-mutilating.

"We infected her two days before you. She has degenerated quite rapidly, as you can see."

When Tian caught sight of the vampire, she snapped to attention. The man was looking at her curiously. I saw his lips move, but she didn't answer. Instead, she began to stalk him, moving quickly around the table. Alarmed by her predatory attitude, he backed away. She toyed with him for a while, gliding from side to side, forcing him to mirror her movements. A cat playing with a mouse.

I knew the minute she grew tired of the game. Her eyes narrowed, her body tensed, and in a blur of motion she leapt across the table to pin him against the wall. He was twice her size and likely three times her weight, but her grip was iron. Under the influence of a blood high, I too had incredible strength and speed. But they paled in comparison to the abilities Tian now possessed.

When her teeth struck his neck, blood spattered the whiteness of the ceiling and ran down the wall to pool on the floor. I watched him scream but heard only the sound of my own ragged breaths. Tian feasted viciously, heedless of the hands that scrabbled against her head in an effort to push her away.

My own throat burned in empathy as I watched her drain him dry, but I couldn't tell whether the mere sight of Tian drinking had further whetted my appetite, or whether I was craving her victim's vampire blood. When he slumped into unconsciousness, she kept his deadweight pinned to the wall. She drank until his body had nothing left to offer, then pried herself away and crouched, shivering, next to the corpse. Clutching her own knees, rocking back and forth, she seemed vulnerable despite what she had just done. Never had I seen a vampire take so much blood at once.

Two huge guards entered the room and one yanked Tian onto her feet. I expected her to attack, but she didn't. They led her away, leaving me to contemplate the gleaming room festooned with crimson trails. I thought of my conversation with Tian—about the respect she cultivated for humanity. Some vampires delighted in behaving like monsters, but she was not one. Was her mind rebelling in the new desires of her body? Or had the parasite effectively colonized her psyche as well as her cells? And when would I feel the transformation in myself?

The door to my room opened and Tian was shoved inside. She had been changed into a new pair of scrubs and her face had been washed. She eyed me warily, arms wrapped around herself.

"Tian." I spoke in the same tone I used whenever Alexa's panther was close to the surface. "It's me, Valentine."

When she blinked, her stare devoid of recognition, I tried again. "We met in Prince George. I was one of the people sent to protect you."

She shuddered, arms dropping to her sides. "Valentine Darrow," she said slowly.

"Yes. That's right." Despite my excitement, I kept my voice soft.

"Brenner. He…" She shook her head, clearly having trouble holding on to her own thoughts. "He changed me."

"He infected us both with the parasite," I said. "How do you feel?"

"It's so strong," she said, her voice taking on an eerie, singsong quality. "The thirst, like a gaping maw in my mind…" She sank onto her cot and began to mutter in Chinese.

Clearly, the hybrid parasite was driving her insane. I watched her for a while, waiting in dread for some sign that my body had succumbed. How would I know? Would a new kind of thirst beset me without warning, or would it slowly, steadily build in the way I was already accustomed? Would I begin to perceive blank spots in my awareness as I slipped periodically into madness? If Tian were lucid, she might be able to answer some of my questions. But when I called her name, she didn't react.

A sudden thought propelled me onto my feet, startling Tian, who snarled and bared her teeth like a feral creature. Slowly, I sank back onto the cot, mollifying her even as I tried to think logically. The very structure of my circulatory system had been altered by the Tear of Isis. What if I were immune to the hybrid parasite? What if my body had fought it off? I couldn't be certain, but if Tian had sunk so low after only two days, surely I would be showing some symptoms already.

Brenner hadn't yet shown his hand, and I couldn't tell whether he intended to use us as weapons or as incubators. If I was correct about my immunity, one simple blood test would reveal that I was useless to his project. At that point, he would either try to kill me or work to find a use for my unique blood structure. But in the short term, if I played along, I might be able to find a way to escape.

For the sake of the act, I allowed my frustration to show. While Tian gnashed her teeth and whispered in her native tongue, I paced the width of the room. I bit at my nail beds. I slammed my fist into the wall. I prayed that Brenner would see what he wanted to see, and that my chance would come.

And above all, I prayed Alexa was safe.

CHAPTER FIFTEEN

I was woken from a fitful doze by the creak of the door. The same two guards entered, accompanied by a man in a white lab coat holding a syringe. As the guards held down a struggling, spitting Tian, I didn't need to fake my own anxiety. The man inserted the needle into her vein, withdrew a tube of blood, and then moved toward me. I scrambled into sitting position, my attention flickering between the two guards as they approached. When they were within my reach I launched myself at one, but the other grabbed hold and forced me onto the bed.

A stinging pain in my own elbow marked their success. But instead of letting me go, the guards hauled me onto my feet and shoved me toward the door. When I tried to resist, they pushed me to my knees and dragged me out into a narrow corridor. Turning my head, I managed to catch a glimpse of Tian, but she hadn't even reacted to my absence. Curled into a near fetal position on the cot, she was cradling the arm from which they'd drawn the blood and humming.

Moments later, I was shoved into the same room in which Tian had drained the hapless vampire hours—or maybe days—before. The blood had been cleaned from its walls and floors, and the lingering scent of bleach burned my nostrils. On the other side of the table, a female vampire crouched low to the ground, her long blond hair matted against her neck. She stared at me in obvious confusion as the guards left and shut the door. I caught a flash of motion behind her head as the windowpane into our holding cell was once again exposed. Through it, Tian stared at me without recognition.

Thoughts firing rapidly, I began to pace along my side of the table. I had to mimic Tian's behavior just enough so as not to raise suspicion, but perhaps there was some way of converting this moment into an escape. In the meanwhile, I pretended to stalk the vampire slowly and carefully, as I had seen Alexa do in her panther form. Even without the increased strength of the parasite, I was stronger and faster than most other vampires by virtue of being the blood prime of my clan. I had no doubt that I would be able to overpower her. The only question that remained was what to do then.

To make this encounter appear real, I would need to bite her. I wasn't concerned about the taste, though during my time spent combing through some of the medical texts in the Consortium library, I had learned that vampire blood carried a particularly repugnant flavor to other vampires. Rather, I was concerned about my soul. Could drinking from this vampire potentially compromise my circulatory system in the same way that drinking from a human might?

"Who are you?" she asked in a thin voice that was trying to sound imposing but only came off as shrill. "What do you want?"

I didn't answer. Even as I hunted her, my brain was rapidly processing and discarding possibilities. The blood of a full vampire was completely transformed by the parasite. If I bit her, my own blood would find nothing in hers to consume. Theoretically, I would be safe.

I was also out of time. Brenner's guards would become suspicious soon, and I had to act. Even hobbled by my injured leg, my sudden burst of speed was too fast for her to repulse. I leapt over the table and pinned her against the wall, tightening my grip when her nails dug into my forearms.

"Help me," I hissed into her ear. And then I clamped my jaws down onto the delicate skin of her neck.

She screamed. The scent of blood filled the air even as its coppery taste filled my mouth, but every cell in my body recoiled.

Wrong—it tasted utterly wrong, like spoiled milk. Jerking backward, I let my revulsion carry me down to the floor, where I did my best to contort my limbs in a series of false convulsions. The vampire's blood dribbled down my chin as I pushed foamy spittle between my lips, and when the door banged hard against the wall I knew my ruse had worked.

I leapt to my feet and took out the first guard with a roundhouse kick. When my wounded leg faltered under my own full weight, I converted my stumble into a forward roll, ducking a brutal blow from a rifle butt. The man I'd knocked down scrambled away in the hopes of taking a shot, but I wrapped my left arm around his legs and knocked the pistol from his hands. I shot him point-blank in the heart, then turned the gun toward the window separating me from Tian.

As the glass shattered I spun in a quick circle, assessing the situation. Someone had activated an alarm, and its rhythmic blare only added to my headache. Blinking rapidly, I worked to channel my adrenaline. I had to stay focused. The vampire whom Brenner had intended to be my victim had a good head on her shoulders and was currently managing to keep both an orderly and another guard occupied. After dispatching the latter with a quick bullet to the head, we took down the guard together.

"Go, go, go!" I shouted, shoving her toward the open door. Behind us, Tian was crouched on a pile of glass splinters, and I beckoned for her to follow.

But when the vampire emerged into the corridor, she was immediately felled by a bullet to the head. Cursing, I scrambled back to the other dead guard and grabbed his weapon. Tian stood a few feet away, looking uncertain, and I shouted for her to follow me. Crouching low in the doorway, feet slipping in the pool of gore, I sprayed bullets both ways and took off running in the opposite direction from where Brenner's men had brought me. When I dared to look over my shoulder, I found Tian at my heels. Every ten feet, I fired a fresh salvo of bullets behind us.

Each time we approached an intersection, our pace slowed as we looked for signs of an ambush. By the time I saw the first red

EXIT sign set into the ceiling, we had already fought off two of Brenner's patrols. Despite the incessant ache in my head and legs, relief swept through me as I shouldered my way through the door. We had our choice of whether to go up or down the stairs, but for once the decision was easy. For this installation to have avoided detection by our satellites, it had to be underground. If we could reach the surface, we might just be able to make a clean escape.

I pounded up the stairs as fast as my injury would allow. The last door let out into a wide corridor that smelled heavily of gasoline. I held up my hand, indicating that we should proceed more slowly. Small rooms to our left and right appeared to be either closets or windowless offices, and we passed them by quickly—until the penultimate door opened and two tall figures dressed in heavy white parkas stepped into the hall. They had been outside recently; tiny bits of ice still clung to the fur collars of the jackets, and their boots squished against the floor. When they turned toward us, I leapt forward and tried to strike the nearer man across the forehead with my pistol, but his reflexes were sharp and the blow was only glancing. Balance compromised, I stumbled across the floor as he reached toward his waist.

Tian crossed the intervening distance in a blur, and her kick to the guard's sternum sent him crashing into the wall. The other guard raised his gun, but she knocked it away with her elbow. Leaping onto his back, she wrapped her arms around his neck in a chokehold that brought him to his knees. He passed out from lack of oxygen just as the first one charged back into the fray, but I was ready and dispatched him with a quick shot to the head. He collapsed to the floor, twitched, and lay still.

❖

The rich, earthy scent of Were blood bloomed on the air and I spun away only to find Tian standing over the motionless form of the other man. Saliva flooded my mouth, and my vision telescoped to the dark red pool spreading behind her assailant's head. Beneath the riptide of my thirst, I realized that I'd been right about my condition. My throat burned with every breath, but it wasn't the blood of a vampire I craved. Clenching my free hand into a fist, I focused my mind's eye on the image of Alexa's face. Alexa. I needed her so badly. Only her. I would not drink from these shifters. I would not. We were so close to freedom, and I had to keep my eye on the prize.

"We need their parkas," I said, hearing the strain in my own voice as I tried to overcome my own bloodlust. "And boots. Hurry."

But instead of obeying, Tian stood motionless and watched me. Cursing under my breath, I hastily pulled on my parka and shoved my feet into a pair of boots several sizes too large before ripping the coat and shoes off her kill and pushing the bundle of clothing into her arms. When I searched the pockets of my parka, my fingers closed around a set of keys. I dangled them between us, taking note of the Jeep insignia on the chain, and for the first time in what felt like an eternity, triumph sang through me.

"We're looking for a Jeep that's been driven recently," I said, starting off again down the hallway.

The corridor ended in a large, windowless door, and we managed to reach it without encountering anyone else. The scent of oil and gas was even stronger here, and after checking to ensure that Tian was behind me, I took a deep breath and opened the door just a crack.

It was a garage. Naked light bulbs hung from the ceiling, casting eerie shadows on the concrete floor. Cars, trucks, and snowcats were parked in neat rows, waiting for use. I couldn't see any guards from this angle, but that didn't mean they weren't present. As quietly as I was able, I slipped through the door and held it open for Tian.

We crept along the periphery, keeping our backs to the walls as much as possible. Every time I saw a Jeep, I moved forward and placed my hand on its hood, testing for warmth. Finally, on my fifth try, I found the vehicle we were looking for.

The sound of a muttered conversation near the front of the garage reached my ears as I jammed the key into the lock and twisted. Tian, still barefoot and carrying her outwear, regarded me blankly as I gestured for her to open her door. Her brief moments of lucidity were quickly becoming few and far between. Biting my lip to keep from cursing, I skirted the outside of the car, opened her door, and gently pushed her into the passenger's seat. Once I'd buckled myself into the driver's side, I scanned the interior of the car for something that would help us get out of here. Some kind of remote control device was clipped to the sun guard. I peered out the windshield, hoping to find a door, but fifty yards away, the garage tapered off into a two-lane tunnel that I presumed led up to the surface. Maybe the entrance at the end of the tunnel was sealed, and this remote would activate the door? Making that assumption could be a fatal error, but we didn't have much of a choice.

I glanced over at Tian, who was staring straight ahead with a glassy-eyed expression and moistening her lips continuously with her tongue. She hadn't put on her seat belt, so I reached over to buckle her in. Setting my gun on my lap, I braced one arm against the wheel and turned the key halfway in the ignition so I could lower the windows.

"This could get ugly," I said, uncertain that she could even hear me. "Shoot anything that moves."

The car roared to life, and I put it in drive and pressed down hard on the accelerator. Tires screeched against concrete and the Jeep shot forward. Over the sound of our acceleration, I heard shouting. I grabbed my weapon, pointed it out the window, and fired blindly in the direction of the sounds even as I guided the car across the open space and into the narrow tunnel. The road began to slope upward almost immediately, and when I switched on the bright lights they illuminated the rock walls and rough asphalt surface of the tunnel. Ready to slam on the brakes at a moment's notice, I curled one hand around the sunshield and pressed the remote in the hopes that I'd activate whatever door was waiting for us from the maximum distance.

"There!" It was the first word Tian had said in hours, and it surprised me so much that at first I didn't see the rising gate several hundred feet ahead, its metal glinting in the scant light that filtered in from outside. I risked a glance down at the clock and saw that it was just after eight o'clock in the morning. Half an hour until sunrise.

"Damn it," I hissed, realizing I'd need to find a way to find a way to shield Tian from the light rather than make a clean escape immediately. But for now, I had to concentrate on making it out of this tunnel, and then on getting as far away as possible from Brenner's installation before we needed to stop.

The car rocketed out into the pre-dawn, and I welcomed the fresh, cold air against my face. Pushing the accelerator down to the mat, I urged the Jeep forward over the cracked and bumpy surface. This was the only road in sight, and quite possibly the only way in and out of Brenner's facility.

What was he doing right now? Would he send vehicles out after us? Airplanes? A chopper? As much as he wanted to remain off the Consortium's radar, I knew he wouldn't simply let us go. The only question was how and when he would come after us. With intimate knowledge of the land and vastly superior resources, he had the clear advantage.

Mile after mile passed without any sign of pursuit, but I only grew more and more tense. Tian seemed to pick up on my restlessness, or perhaps she was reacting to the proximity of daylight. She fidgeted in her seat, face and hands pressed to the glass of her window. At first, I tried to tell her about my plan to find us both shelter before the sun rose, but she only peered at me intently before turning back to her contemplation of the landscape, and I suspected she was now beyond hearing.

The road began to climb, twisting around rocky outcroppings as we ascended into a line of hills. As we ascended, the land fell away until we were driving along a narrow ridge, sheer cliffs dropping into the valley on both sides. Tension burned in my shoulders as I divided my attention between the road ahead and the sky above, searching for signs of pursuit.

Suddenly, a sharp cracking sound against the passenger side window made me momentarily lose my grip on the wheel, and the car swerved first left, then right. Heart pounding, I risked a glance at Tian only to suck in a sharp breath in horror as she pounded her head and fists against the glass. When I grabbed her arm, she spun to face me, blood streaming down her cheeks. Its pungent, metallic scent turned my stomach.

"Tian! Stop! What are you—"

Curling her fingers into the shape of a claw, she pierced the skin on the back of my hand as she forced me away. Drops of my blood welled up into the air, and finally, epiphany struck. Tian had been fighting herself this entire time. She was thirsty, and she wanted to drink *me*.

My thoughts collided chaotically as I tried to process what was happening and determine what to do about it. How had she resisted her appetite for so long? Was it because the flower in my blood made me different? Because she had fed only a short time ago? Or because she still retained a shred of her legendary self-control? And how was I going to save her if she wanted to tear me to pieces?

"Tian. You can fight this. I know you can. I'll pull over soon, just—"

I could sense the precise moment she lost control. Her every muscle tensed, and darkness swallowed the whites of her eyes. As the thirst overpowered her, she lunged for me. In desperation, I spun the wheel violently to the right and then to the left. The car swerved sharply, knocking her off balance just enough so I could grab the pistol and smash it hard against her temple. Dazed and reeling, she fell forward into the dashboard.

I looked up to the sight of the sunrise. In a burst of flame that set the wispy cirrus clouds ablaze, the sun climbed up over the horizon. And then I realized that the Jeep was seconds away from vaulting off the cliff and into space, and that there was nothing I could possibly do to change our trajectory.

Desperately, I shoved at the door handle with one hand and slammed my other fist down onto the seat belt lock, then threw myself out of the car. As I slammed into the ground, the breath was knocked from my chest and my injured leg screamed in protest. The scenery passed by in dizzying glimpses: jagged rock, deep snow drifts, a winding road. The ground raced up to meet me. Pain shot through both shoulders and down along my spine. I screamed, and then I was falling again.

Coldness caught me, cushioned me, held me. Whiteness filled my eyes, my ears, my mouth. For a moment, I was at peace, as though I had landed on a cloud. And then the explosion shattered the silence, roaring its fury to the heavens while the earth rolled beneath me in protest.

I sat up slowly, testing out each limb in turn. My lower back felt as though it were on fire, and my stomach roiled whenever I moved my head too quickly. Otherwise, I seemed remarkably unscathed. Blinking the moisture out of my eyes, I took stock of my surroundings. I'd rolled several dozen feet down a steep incline. Thankfully, instead of going over the cliff, I'd been lucky enough to fall into a snow bank, where my landing had carved out a sizeable hollow. But when I tried to scramble to my feet, I only sank further.

I got on my belly instead, army crawling my way up until I reached a point where the snow was packed firmly enough to bear my weight. As soon as I rose to my knees, I saw the crash site. Black smoke billowed above the flames devouring the twisted body of the Jeep. Metal shrapnel littered the snow for a hundred feet, marking the path where the vehicle had skidded. No one could have survived the crash, and I felt a swift surge of grief that Tian had come to such an end.

Tian. The Blood Prime of the Sunrunners—arguably the most powerful vampire in the world—was dead. Perhaps it was a blessing. The hybrid parasite had decimated her will and her psyche. Mindless with thirst, her brief moments of lucidity had been shot through with pain. Doubtless, her death had been mercifully quick.

Cold water trickled down into my boots, soaking my ankles and feet and reminding me of my predicament. My grief would have to wait until I had managed to get myself to safety. I wouldn't last long in the middle of this wilderness. Before me, the wilderness stretched white and forbidding, but in the distance I caught sight of a massive black snake winding toward the horizon. A highway— much larger than the road we'd been on. Between it and me stretched a hundred feet of vertical cliff and, if I had to guess, a mile of snow-covered plain. But there was no way I could climb down a nearly sheer rock face in my present condition. I would have to follow the access road for a while longer, until I could find a suitable place to climb down.

Laboriously, I clambered back up the way I'd fallen. My feet sank only a few inches with each step and I set a brisk pace toward the road. Already, my toes were growing dangerously cold. There was no way I could avoid some degree of frostbite, but the more quickly I got to the highway, the less likelihood I had of damaging myself irrevocably.

The wind whistled around me, chapping my face. Above, wispy clouds the color of cotton candy scudded across a slowly brightening sky. The sunrise was magnificent, and I found myself hoping that some part of Tian had been able to appreciate it—the first she'd seen in centuries—in the moments before her death.

After about half a mile of walking along the pockmarked surface of the access road, I found an incline shallow enough to scramble down. Pulling my hands into the sleeves of the parka, I half-slipped, half-slid down the icy, rocky slope. By the time I reached the bottom, my tailbone was bruised and frozen. To distract myself from the searing pain in my back and the slow burn of my feet, I imagined how it would feel to ride across this landscape in a sled pulled by a team of magnificent huskies, Alexa at my side. To skate over the ice and under the sky, to feel the strength of the dogs and hear their joyous barking, to find warmth in each other at night...it would be glorious.

I was so focused on maintaining my forward trajectory that when my foot struck solid ground I tripped, and my right knee crashed down hard. Gritting my teeth against the stabbing pain, it took me several seconds to register what my torn scrubs and bruised skin indicated. Asphalt. I had reached the highway.

As the minutes passed without any sign of a vehicle, I began to shiver. My feet felt like blocks of ice, and my soaked-through pants were only making my condition worse. And then, just as I was about to start doing calisthenics in an effort to stay warm, headlights appeared on the horizon.

I stood in the middle of the highway, removed my parka, and began to wave it like a flag, hoping that some part of it would reflect off the oncoming lights. The distant roar of the engine diminished slightly, and I realized two things: the oncoming vehicle was a freighter, and its driver might have just seen the smoke still billowing skyward from the Jeep's crash.

The truck approached and I kept waving until the last possible moment before jumping off to the side. It continued on, and as I watched it go, dejection made my shoulders slump...until the screech of its brakes filled the air. Elation propelled my sore and weary legs into a brisk walk, but as I approached the driver's side of the cab, I wondered just how bad I looked.

The window descended, and as I stepped closer, the portly man behind the wheel gaped at me. "Were you in an accident? The smoke—"

"Yes," I interrupted, pitching my voice low to ensure that I'd pass as a man. "My Jeep crashed. I'm fine, but I really need a ride to the nearest town."

"Sure, boss, sure." The driver seemed excited to be able to help. Maybe he thought I'd offer him some kind of reward, or that he'd make the news and become a famous hero. "Hop on board."

I climbed in the passenger's side, closed the door, and lunged for him. He struggled against my grip, but despite my depleted strength, I held him easily. As my hand clenched around his throat to cut off his oxygen, I couldn't help but focus on his pulsing jugular vein. Saliva flooded my mouth, and my throat burst into flame. His blood would be hot and viscous and sweet on my tongue. It would fill me up, warm me up, make me strong. I needed it. Now.

With a Herculean effort, I jerked back into the passenger seat, panting with need. No. I had no idea how long I'd been in Brenner's captivity, but I could wait a few more hours. Or even longer, if necessary. I had sworn to Alexa that I would never again betray her, and I would keep that promise, especially now. I could wait. I *would* wait.

Clenching my teeth against my thirst, I inventoried the cab. In the space behind the seats, I found a suitcase, a toolbox, and a cooler. From the suitcase, I grabbed socks, a pair of sweats, and a sweatshirt and quickly stripped off my icy clothes. Once I had changed, I took off the man's sneakers and put them on, then tied his hands and legs with duct tape from the toolbox. After pocketing his keys, cell phone, and cash, I opened the trailer and arranged him among his freight, adding a piece of tape across his mouth to keep him quiet.

The truck was a fairly new model with a built-in GPS, and I quickly took stock of my position as soon as I returned to the cab. Right now, I was two hundred miles northeast of Fairbanks, which meant that Brenner's base was twenty miles or so farther north. I took note of the GPS coordinates, repeating them under my breath until I had committed them to memory.

After a quick inspection of the gears, I got the truck underway. Any minute now, another vehicle could appear on the horizon and I couldn't risk them stopping to check on me. For the first few minutes, I accustomed myself to the gears, the brakes, the tightness of the steering. Once I was pointed south on a long, straight stretch, I reached for the trucker's phone and plugged his headphones into my ears.

Anticipation and anxiety flooded through me as I punched in Alexa's cell number. Her phone might have been lost during our scouting mission to the hangar, but surely she would have gotten a new one. As long as they had all made it back. But no. No. I couldn't think like that. She had survived. I had to believe it. My hands trembled as I hit the "call" button.

One ring. Two. Three. My heart stuttered as hope faltered. What if—

"Hello?"

When I heard her voice, I realized part of me had despaired of ever hearing it again. I wanted to laugh. I wanted to cry. She was in pain. Even those two simple syllables had sounded so tired. Defeated.

I tried to speak and failed.

"Hello?" Irritation and suspicion crept in behind her fatigue. "Who is this?"

"Baby." I finally croaked out the word.

Silence. I swallowed desperately, throat tight with unshed tears. "Alexa? It's me."

"Valentine?" She spoke my name incredulously, and I could hear the tears in her voice. Answering moisture cascaded down my own cheeks.

"Yes, love. Yes. It's me. I'm so glad you're okay."

"Val, my God, I can't believe I'm—we've been out of our minds with—where are you?"

"In a truck two hundred miles northeast of Fairbanks. I'm driving back to the safe house as we speak. Did everyone…make it back? From the hangar?"

"Yes. We've been combing the area around that airfield since you were taken, but every lead has been a dead-end." She paused to take a deep breath. "Val, did Brenner…succeed?"

"He did. He infected Tian, but it didn't work on me. Tian is dead, love. She died during our escape."

For several seconds, she didn't speak. "This is insane. God, Val, I was so scared. So, so damn scared."

"I know. Me, too. I thought I'd never see you again." I swiped at my eyes, letting the sound of her rhythmic breaths comfort me. "How long has it been since that night?"

"Five days."

My mind struggled to assimilate the news that I had only been in captivity for less than a week. "It felt like a year."

I heard her swallow hard. "How badly did he hurt you?"

"Nothing that won't heal. But I need you."

"Do you want us to meet you half way?"

I shook my head, even though she couldn't see me. "No. You're going to be needed there. Have Malcolm pull surveillance data from the Alaska interior. The closest town to my position is called Central. Brenner's base is about twenty miles to the north."

"You don't want us to just meet you there?" she asked.

"No. It's too close. He'll catch wind of us. Right now, I'm ninety percent certain he thinks I'm dead, which gives us some time to formulate a concrete plan."

"Okay." When she spoke again, her voice was thick with unshed tears. "I still can't believe I'm talking to you, Val. This whole week has felt like a nightmare."

The distraught tone of her voice made my heart ache. "I know, baby, I know. But it's all going to be okay. I promise."

For a few moments, neither of us said a word, content simply to listen to the sound of the other breathing. But finally, Alexa sighed.

"I should go. This place is about to turn into even more of a madhouse."

"I know. I love you."

"And I love you," she said. "More than anything."

When the call disconnected, I couldn't help feeling bereft. But that was ridiculous. Within a few hours, we would be reunited. Until then, all I had to do was stay alert and guide the truck safely to Fairbanks. Glancing in the rearview mirror, I caught sight of my face. I was deathly pale and my eyes looked like dark bruises. I had clearly lost weight. Exhaustion thrummed behind my eyes, but I refused to acknowledge its pull. Rest would have to wait until I reached the city.

Chapter Sixteen

It was late in the afternoon by the time I pulled onto the shoulder of the road just outside the entrance to the estate and cut the engine. The last hour of the drive had been a constant battle to keep my eyes open, and I wanted to collapse. Malnourished and dehydrated in two different ways, my energy stores were in serious need of replenishing.

Within moments, a semicircle of armed guards was ringed around the cab of the truck. Unsure of how to respond, I raised my hands into the air. I didn't recognize any familiar faces, and while I was certain they'd been told to expect me, they were also right to be suspicious. One of the men opened the driver's side door.

"Who are you?"

"Valentine Darrow, Missionary and Blood Prime."

The one who seemed to be in charge extended the same kind of portable fingerprint reader Tian's servants had used.

"For verification."

When I pressed my thumb to the screen, I noticed my hand was shaking. Frowning, I concentrated on steadying my grip until the tremor had disappeared. When the device chirped, the man nodded.

"Thank you, Missionary. Welcome. Our orders are to escort you to the command center. A car awaits you just inside the gate."

"This truck and its driver need to be dealt with," I said as I climbed down from the cab. My legs screamed in protest, and as I hobbled through the gate, I finally gave up trying not to betray any weakness. "Humanely, please. I want him to have all of his assets intact. Just not his memories of the last several hours."

"I understand, Missionary."

As I slid my aching muscles into the backseat of the waiting Range Rover, a strong fatigue swept over me, rendering me dizzy. I focused on taking deep, steady breaths, but the sensation of vertigo never completely dissipated. Had I reached the limits of my superhuman body? Brenner had withheld food and water for days, but that deprivation was only exacerbating my condition, not causing it. I needed Alexa's blood—my greatest strength and my greatest weakness. Soon. Leaning my head against the window, I watched the tops of the bare trees dance to the beat of a chill wind as the car drew steadily closer to the safe house.

We parked directly in front of the entrance and I got out of the car on unsteady legs, feeling like an octogenarian. Suddenly, the front door was being thrown open and Alexa—too thin, too pale, and dressed in black camo—was flying down the stairs. She skidded to a halt in front of me, her face a kaleidoscope of emotions. Love, anger, fear, worry—they lashed at her like gale force winds. I tried to smile, but my face didn't seem to be working properly. I tried to walk into her arms, but suddenly my legs wouldn't bear my own weight.

Without any warning, I finally succumbed to the tidal wave of my exhaustion. As it pulled me under, I collapsed into her embrace.

❖

Gentle hands stroked my back as loving words filled my ears. I breathed in deeply, smiling as I filled my lungs with her scent. Alexa. Home. Safe.

"Val, love, I know you're so tired. But can you wake up for me, just for a little while? Please?"

I wanted to make her happy, but my limbs wouldn't work properly. They were impossibly heavy. Even my eyelids had been immobilized by tiny weights.

"Can't," I murmured, already on the verge of falling back to sleep.

"Did you catch that?" Alexa said. She sounded far away.

"I think she said, 'can't.'" A familiar voice. Karma.

"I've never seen her virtually unresponsive like this."

Alexa sounded frightened. I wanted to tell her that everything was going to be just fine, but my lips wouldn't form the words.

"What do you think is wrong?" asked Karma.

"I know exactly what she needs. I've just never seen her too weak to take it for herself."

I heard the rustling of cloth, and then the mattress moved beneath me as someone else added their weight to the bed. Alexa or Karma? I wanted to open my eyes to see. When I tried and failed, irritation seeped through my lethargy. A frustrated groan caught at the back of my throat.

"What was that?" said Karma.

"I think she's trying," said Alexa. "Hand me that knife, please. I'll meet you downstairs as soon as I can."

"You're sure you don't want me to stay?"

"She's been through hell and she's starving in more ways than one. I need to remind her of us. She won't hurt me, Karma."

Alexa sounded so confident—so sure of herself, and of our relationship. She was my champion. She fought so hard. Wasn't she tired? I wanted to tug her down next to me on the bed and wrap my arms around her and bury my face in her hair and sleep for years.

"I understand. Be safe."

The door shut. Alexa's hands were gentle as she turned me onto my back. I wanted to see her face, but my eyes refused to open.

"I love you, Valentine." As she spoke the words, the air became redolent with the aroma of heaven—rich and fragrant and pure. She grasped the back of my head and pressed her skin to my lips. "Drink. Come back to me."

The first taste unlocked my frozen body. As the gift of her blood trickled into my parched throat, my eyes flew open to the sight of her face, fierce and loving, above me. She had opened her wrist for me, and I reached up to clutch at her arm.

"Yes, Val," she gasped as I pulled deeply from her vein, filling myself with the heat and brightness of her. She flowed into me, pouring her strength into my aching muscles, knitting together my broken skin, soothing my bruised soul.

"I love you," she whispered, eyes locked on mine. "I love you."

I drank and drank, losing myself in her intoxicating taste, glorying in the vitality that returned to my body and mind. I never wanted to stop, but as my lucidity returned so did my sense of priority. Gentling my mouth against her, I licked the small wounds until I felt her skin close beneath my tongue.

When I rolled onto my side and pulled her down to face me, she traced the lines of my face with tender strokes of her fingertips. I had despaired of ever seeing her again, and every loving touch was bliss.

"Thank you," I said, leaning in to press my lips to her tremulous smile. Her mouth opened to me like a flower, soft and delicate, and despite the demands weighing down on us I let myself luxuriate in the kiss.

Finally, we parted. She rubbed her thumb across my mouth and I let my fingers sift through her hair, marveling at the crispness of the world. As I pushed myself into sitting position, I realized that already, I was experiencing far less pain than I had hours ago.

"How do you feel?" she asked, mimicking my position on the bed.

"You're a miracle," I told her. "I was near comatose, wasn't I?"

"It did seem that way." She wouldn't meet my eyes. "You didn't feed at all, while we were apart?"

Her insecurity pierced me, and I cradled her hands in mine. "I think Brenner wanted to keep me hungry. I had a close moment with the truck driver, but then I thought of you and how I never wanted to betray you again, and I was able to stay in control. Whatever the flower did to my blood, I think it's helped me with that."

My declaration only seemed to agitate her. She stood and began to pace. "Damn it, your body just shut down. I don't ever want to stand in the way of what you need to survive."

I blocked her path, grasped her shoulders, and pulled her into my embrace. "Alexa, *you* are what I need to survive. Only you. I made it. We're together, and thanks to you I'm already healing." I cupped her face, compelling her to meet my gaze. "Now it's time to finish what Brenner started—to take the opportunity to be rid of him so we can live in peace."

She swallowed hard, then nodded. "You're right."

"Are the others downstairs? I want to tell them everything I know. Maybe some of it will help as we formulate a plan."

"Yes. When I left them, they were planning to review intelligence reports of the area you clued us into."

I reached for her hand, twining our fingers together. "Then let's go."

But she resisted. "You didn't take very much from me. There's no way you're even close to full strength, after what you've just been through."

I leaned in to kiss her all too briefly. "You're right. Which is why once I've finished briefing everyone, I'm going to drag you back up here." I smoothed a finger over the dark smudges beneath her eyes. "You need to rest, too."

We found the remainder of the team gathered in the mansion's spacious living room. Foster was hunched over a laptop, speaking with someone—presumably at Headquarters—in hushed tones. Karma, Constantine, and Malcolm were poring over maps spread out across the coffee table and floor. They all looked up as I entered, and Foster ended her call.

Karma jumped up to embrace me, and Foster stood to give me a one-armed hug. As Alexa and I sat on the couch, Constantine reached over to squeeze my hand, and even Malcolm smiled.

"Any luck?" I asked, indicating the maps.

"We've identified a few possibilities," said Constantine. "Nothing definite yet."

"Any information you can share would be helpful," Malcolm said, surprising me with his almost deferential tone. Perhaps the fact that I'd managed to escape from Brenner's clutches trumped the distaste he'd felt for me ever since learning that Alexa had chosen to become a wereshifter in order to sustain me forever.

But just as I was about to recount what had happened in Brenner's lair, a surge of anxiety made it difficult to speak. My heartbeat accelerated as the panic rolled over my brain like a dark fog, and suddenly, I was back in that white room, bound to the steel table, spread open and helpless—

The warm pressure of Alexa's hand on my leg pulled me back from the darkness. The room was silent, save for my labored breaths. Ashamed, I stared at my fists, clenched white-knuckled on my knees.

Alexa kissed my jaw. "You're all right, my love. I'm here. You're among friends."

I calmed my breathing and cleared my throat. Alexa was right. I didn't have to look into the void alone, and that made all the difference.

Between their questions and several interruptions from Headquarters and Malcolm's scouts, it took me almost two hours to tell the full story. By the time I had finished, exhaustion had crept back into my every cell.

"We have to assume that he is manufacturing the cannibal parasite as fast as possible for widespread distribution." Malcolm's large hands balled into fists on the table.

In my mind, I flashed back to Tian, crazed in her thirst for vampire blood. To imagine a vampire civil war perpetrated by legions of starving, mindless killers was beyond horrible. For a moment, I was glad that Tian had perished so she wouldn't see the Armageddon that was coming. The tragic betrayal of her own parasite DNA.

"Do you think he might already have weaponized it?" I asked. "Do we know if Brenner's still here?"

"Our people have been closely monitoring the air traffic out of the Alaska interior for the past five days," said Malcolm. "We've been able to account for all passengers in and out of the region, and none of them were Brenner."

"That's no guarantee that he's still at the installation," Constantine chimed in. "He could have left by car or he could be four-legged. But that would still put him in the general vicinity."

I nodded, discouragement adding to my fatigue. We were adding up what-ifs, not certainties. They could easily amount to nothing.

"Okay. Enough." Alexa got to her feet and extended her hand to me. "We're going to get some rest." Her tone brooked no argument, and no one made to stop us. "Until there's a plan, or a question only Val can answer, we're out of commission."

She kept her arm around my waist as we ascended the stairs, but when she would have immediately pulled me into bed, I resisted.

"I need to take a shower."

"You're fine, sweetheart. Let's just crawl under the—"

"No!" My vehemence surprised me, and I dropped my eyes to the floor. "I'm a mess, and…and after talking about all that, I just want to be clean again."

"Okay," she said softly. "I understand. Can I join you?" When I nodded, she smiled and told me to raise my arms. As she undressed me, she pressed a kiss to every scrape, every bruise. She treated my aching body with the utmost care, and instead of feeling weak, I only felt cherished.

"You're beautiful, Valentine. Bruised and battered, yes, but still so beautiful. Now, pay attention."

Alexa stripped slowly. As I watched her peel off each successive layer of clothing, desire welled up in my chest, over-spilling its bounds until it cascaded through every vein and vessel. She made me feel so alive, and I relaxed into my arousal, my thirst, my love for her. They braided together to become *need*—all encompassing need that blazed through my every cell.

With a smile, she went into the bathroom and turned on the shower, adjusting the temperature until steam billowed out into the room.

"Come on, sweetheart." She took my hand and led me inside, wincing in sympathy at my hiss of pain as the water struck my abrasions. I fell into a daze as her fingertips massaged my scalp, as her palms swept gently over my body. She cleaned the grime and blood from my skin, and as I watched the shampoo and soap run down my legs and into the drain, I imagined my fears and anxieties following suit.

Once I was clean, she began to wash herself, but I snapped out of my daze and took the bar of soap from her hands. I whispered to her as I washed her, telling her how much I loved her, how much I had missed her, my hands lathering her thick hair and kneading the muscles of her back and lingering on her full breasts.

We dried off quickly and fell onto the bed, everything forgotten except each other. When I moved to slide my body over hers, Alexa pulled me beneath her with a strength I could not resist.

"No," she whispered, eyes shining with love but her face fierce with need. "I almost lost you, Valentine. You know what that feels like—so dark, so empty. And now you're here, you're safe, and I need to fill myself up with you. Don't deny me that."

"Never," I gasped, the intensity of her words making me liquid with desire. "I would never deny you anything."

She cradled my face as she kissed me, our bodies cleaving together. As I stroked the long muscles of her back and the curve of her buttocks, she raised her head and shuddered for breath.

"Your hands on me feel so, so good."

"I love you," I said and tried to recapture her lips. But she had other plans.

Her mouth skated along my jaw line, then down the column of my neck. The closer she moved to my breasts, the more incandescent I became, my harsh breaths echoing loudly throughout the room.

"I love the sounds you make. How responsive you are for me." She flicked her tongue across my nipple, and her name left my mouth on a low moan.

As she lavished attention on my breasts, my capacity for thought deserted me, swept away on the tide of arousal she had created. My body melted beneath her and my groans became incoherent. I was need incarnate.

Her mouth remained at my breast as one hand slipped lower, bumping across my ribs before stroking along my abdomen. And then her fingers found me, and my hips rose to meet her touch as pleasure flared along every nerve.

"You feel amazing, Val," she whispered, never pausing her soft strokes as she slid farther down my body.

When I felt the warmth of her breath against me, I shuddered and forced my eyes open. She stared back at me, smiling, exultant. "I want to be inside you, Valentine."

"Yes. Please, yes." My breath caught as she poised one finger to enter me, then slowly, carefully increased the pressure.

"Oh, God," she groaned. "You're so tight." She pushed, and my body clenched around her fingertip. "Open, my love. Be open for me. I want all of you."

She bent her head, and as the heat of her mouth closed around me, she slid deep inside my body. My mouth opened on a soundless scream as the ecstasy found me, possessed me, wrung me out. Alexa stayed with me through it all, coaxing every ounce of pleasure, every drop of release from my body.

Finally, she withdrew, sliding up along my side to wrap her arms around me. She kissed the corner of my mouth, my cheek, my earlobe. "That was incredible. I love you, Valentine."

Her declaration galvanized me, and I fought past the lassitude that suffused my body to roll her beneath me. Her eyes were wide and dark, her breathing quick. Now that she had had her fill of me, she craved my touch.

The confidence was heady. Bracing my weight on my elbows, I plunged my hands into her hair and tilted her head back, exposing her throat. She shuddered against me, and as I pressed my thigh between her legs, I felt her wetness coat my skin.

"Mine," I growled, nipping gently at her breasts, her collarbone, her neck, teasing her without breaking skin.

She reached up to pull my right hand down to the juncture of her thighs. "Yes," she hissed. "Take me, Val. Make me yours."

Refusing to be commanded, I teased her first, swirling my fingertips against her most sensitive skin and kissing the breathy pleas from her lips. She grew more and more insistent until at last I gave in, plunging two fingers deep inside her body, glorying in her ecstatic cry and the clench of her muscles around me.

I thrust slowly at first, then faster and faster until I felt her grow impossibly tight around my knuckles. Finally, I slid my teeth into her neck and she exploded, bucking and shivering, her passion igniting every corner of my soul.

It was so hard to withdraw—to ease my teeth and my touch from the welcoming embrace of her body—but I didn't want to deplete her much more than I already had. She blinked up at me in sleepy satisfaction as I smoothed her damp hair back from her face.

"I love when you look at me like that," I said.

"Mm, like what?"

"Like I'm some kind of demigod."

She laughed and rolled onto her side, fitting her body into the curve of mine. "If I say that you are, will it go to your head?"

I nuzzled her hair and closed my eyes, content to surrender to the pull of my exhaustion. But as I was sliding into sleep, a knock came at the door. I blinked and began to sit up, but Alexa stopped me with a hand between my breasts.

"It's Karma. I'll get it."

I watched her as she answered the door. She was unashamed of her own nudity in that way only wereshifters could be.

"We have a game plan," Karma said. "Do you think Val will be mission ready by tomorrow night?"

"Whether she is or not, she'll insist on going. What time?"

"We're briefing in the morning. Oh-nine hundred hours."

"Thanks," Alexa said. "We'll be there. You'll get some rest, too?"

"I'm going right now."

When Alexa climbed back into my embrace, I kissed her neck. "I guess our people must think they've found the installation."

"And Malcolm's not wasting any time. I'm glad." She stroked the back of my hand. "Do you feel up for it? Going back there, I mean?"

I tightened my grip on her. "I want to go back. Brenner and I have unfinished business."

She spun to face me. "Promise me you won't take any unnecessary risks."

"That's an easy promise to make, as long as you do the same."

She nodded, sliding one leg between mine as she snuggled even closer. "I promise," she murmured. "Whatever happens, we'll face it together."

Chapter Seventeen

The plan was simple, really, I reflected as I pulled on my parachute. Maybe too simple. We wouldn't know for sure until we were in the thick of things, and by then it would be too late to adjust.

The success of this mission depended entirely on our having the element of surprise—a reasonable assumption at this point, but one that could still quite easily blow up in our faces. Once Malcolm had pinned down the location of Brenner's base, he had made the decision to go in with a small strike force first rather than mount a large-scale invasion right away.

I agreed with his logic completely, and I wouldn't have missed being a part of the team for the world. We would be the surgeon's scalpel, swift and precise. As I double-, then triple-checked my chute, I reminded myself of the many missions for which this method had worked beautifully. As much as it had a chance to backfire, I admired the plan's all-or-nothing approach. Either we would succeed or we would die.

I tapped Alexa on the shoulder to get her attention over the loud drone of the propellers. "Let me check your chute!"

Once I was satisfied that nothing was tangled, I turned so she could return the favor. A few moments later, she spun me around and gave me the thumbs-up.

"How are you feeling?" she shouted.

I returned the thumbs-up. We'd had a full night of sleep prior to the briefing, and before we left she'd convinced me to drink from her again. My full-body muscle pain was gone, and I felt alert and strong. My only point of weakness was my leg injury, and we had wrapped it up as well as we could without compromising my range of motion. Still, parachuting out of a plane into enemy territory was probably not on the recommended list of activities while recovering from a leg wound.

"ETA five minutes," Foster called. I pulled on my infrared goggles and clipped to the line just behind Alexa. We had been skydiving once, fairly early in our relationship. The experience had been exhilarating, but it certainly hadn't prepared me for this kind of maneuver.

The jump was going to be tricky even for those who were very experienced. We were aiming for a large air duct that was one of the only aboveground structures of Brenner's installation. It would almost certainly be guarded, and we needed to dispatch whatever sentries he had posted without alerting the main facility. Once inside, we would follow the duct into the center of the facility. From there, we would be on our own.

The jump doors opened and freezing air streamed into the hold. Malcolm stepped out into the night, and ten seconds later Constantine followed him. When it was Alexa's turn, she squeezed my hand, then jumped. It wasn't difficult to throw myself after her. I would have followed her anywhere.

The stars wheeled above me as I plummeted earthward, and I focused on keeping a steady count in my head. Just as I reached "four one-thousand," my shoulders were yanked backward and up as the static line activated my chute. Willing away the pain, I focused on steering toward the infrared beacon that the Consortium intelligence agents had dropped a hundred yards north of the air duct.

My landing wasn't nearly as graceful as it could have been, but I didn't make too much noise and I didn't injure myself any further. After abandoning my chute on the ground, I raced to join the rest of the team.

"You okay?" I asked Alexa quietly as we waited for Karma, who had brought up the rear.

"That was great!" she whispered. "When this is all over, we should go skydiving again."

Before I could reply, Malcolm motioned us forward. We fanned out, crouching low as we made our way up a slight rise, but no guards appeared in our field of view. While Constantine removed the grate over the duct and disabled the fan, we kept watch. I thumbed off the safeties on both of my silenced pistols, surprised that Brenner didn't have a sentry posted out here. Then again, to his knowledge this base was still a tightly kept secret.

The vent sloped down steeply for several yards before flattening out. With Malcolm in the lead, we split the difference between moving quickly and maintaining a quiet approach. Each time we reached a branch, he paused to reevaluate where the strongest breeze was coming from. The outlet with the largest fan would, he had reasoned in our briefing, be located in the place requiring the most ventilation—the main laboratory in the complex. From there, we would systematically search in a spiral pattern until we located Brenner.

It took us fifteen minutes to reach the end of the line. We would have to drop in almost vertically, and we paused for several minutes to determine whether the room below was guarded. While Constantine spider-climbed down to disable the second fan, I pulled down my goggles. Unless someone cut the power, they would no longer be useful.

The vent's protective covering creaked loudly as Constantine removed it, but the rest of our descent was silent. We found ourselves in a rectangular, dimly lit room containing rows of lab benches, four separate fume hoods, and several large refrigerators. I wondered whether the hybrid parasite samples were stored there, and I almost suggested that we check. But the more time we remained stationary, the more likely we were to be discovered. Brenner was the mastermind. Our mission was to cut the head off the snake.

A noise in the hall made us scatter and take cover. From beneath one of the lab benches, I watched the door open. Maybe the guards had been on a regular patrol, or perhaps they had heard some sign of our entry. There were two, and once they stepped inside, they stood no chance.

I rose, gun extended, and shot the left guard in the center of his forehead before he could do more than widen his eyes. Foster was a hairsbreadth slower, and her shot caught the right guard in the shoulder as he began to draw his own weapon. Constantine finished him off neatly. He and I searched their bodies and came up with two keycards.

"Let's go." Malcolm turned right out of the laboratory, and we fanned out on either side of the corridor. I stayed behind Alexa, straining my enhanced senses for any sign of life nearby.

We turned right again before Malcolm paused at a T. I heard him conferring with Constantine and began to approach them in case I could help…only to be brought up short as I passed close to the left-hand opening. A visceral scent memory flooded through me: pain, rage, helplessness. I had been in that corridor. I couldn't remember exactly when, or even if I had been conscious, but I was beyond certain.

"Val?" Alexa's voice was nearly inaudible. "You're trembling. What's wrong?"

"I've been in that hallway." As I pointed left, I drew Malcolm's attention.

"You're sure?"

"Yes, but the memory isn't clear. I don't know what's down there."

"We may as well try it," said Constantine. "Otherwise, we'll be choosing at random."

As we made our way down the corridor, I took deep, even breaths to settle my stomach. I hated this feeling of weakness that had nothing to do with my body and everything to do with my brain. Easing my left-hand pistol out of its holster, I clutched both grips with a feverish intensity, silently daring Brenner and his cronies to test us.

At the end of the corridor, a large door was covered by a metallic grate—the modern equivalent of a portcullis.

"That looks important," Constantine said dryly. "Let's see if this works." He slid the card through the slot in the keypad to the right of the door. A green light blinked, but nothing happened.

"We should have asked for their codes before we shot them," I said, mirroring his tone.

"Do we use our explosives here?" asked Alexa. "Or continue exploring?"

"We should use them," said Malcolm. "This level of protection is a promising sign. Karma?"

"I agree." She set down her rifle, unzipped the large pocket on her vest, and extracted two spheres of plastique. From a different pocket, she produced the detonators. With Constantine's help, she set the charges, and as he lit the fuse we retreated quickly down the hall.

I crouched next to Alexa, shielding us both from the blast. No sooner had the initial shockwave passed than we were in motion. Karma sprayed the smoking threshold with her assault rifle, then leapt inside and continued shooting. I dove through the doorway and halted my momentum in a somersault, searching for enemies as my head came up.

At a flash of tawny fur to my left, I fired twice, felling a large mountain lion. As the smoke began to clear, I realized that we had entered a room full of cubicles. Some of their occupants had shifted, while others remained in human form and were returning fire. Alexa had wedged herself into a well-protected spot between the wall and one of the cubes and was systematically picking soldiers off with her shotgun. Karma continued to lay down cover fire until Constantine charged up the center of the room, his own guns blazing. As I watched, an enemy bullet caught him in the thigh, but he shifted effortlessly and darted to the left.

Karma let loose with another spray of bullets and Malcolm slipped in behind her, picking off those who dared to raise their heads too soon. As the enemy fire temporarily ground to a halt, I darted over to Alexa. She went low, I went high, and together we began to clear the left side of the room.

The acrid scent of gunpowder burned my throat and set my eyes to watering. Struggling to focus through the haze, I suddenly found myself knocked to the ground, left arm stinging as though a swarm of bees had descended upon it at once. I looked down to the sight of a bloody furrow perpendicular to my biceps where a bullet had grazed me. Alexa was leaning over me and asking me if I was okay, and in the midst of all the chaos, I pushed myself up to kiss her. And then I scrambled to my feet, reentering the fray.

Slowly but steadily, we gained ground. As I rounded the corner between the last row of cubicles and the wall, I noticed that the only door set into that wall had been left ajar.

"Cover me!" I shouted to Alexa and made a break for it.

I slid into the room, both weapons extended, heedless of the pain in my arm. The room was empty, but when I took a deep breath, I knew exactly whose office this was. I would never forget the scent of Brenner's musk, and it conjured up the image of his sneering face looming over me, his taunting words echoing in my ears. Even now, I could hear his voice, tormenting me with descriptions of what he would do to Alexa.

And then my blood froze as I realized I wasn't hearing his voice in my head. He was speaking. Right now. Directly outside. Heart racing, I crept behind the door, hoping to catch him in my line of sight. Instead, I saw Malcolm, Karma, and Foster slowly lowering their weapons to the ground.

"Come out of there, Valentine," Brenner called, his voice devoid of any inflection. "I saw you go into my office, and if you don't slide both your firearms out here and crawl into my sight, I'm going to put a bullet through your pretty little girlfriend's brain."

Alexa. He had Alexa. The one thing I'd sworn would never happen, the one thing I had vowed I'd give my life to prevent, had come to pass.

My mind was a blizzard of rage but I did his bidding, pushing both pistols out through the door and then following them on my hands and knees. He had Alexa in a tight headlock, his pistol digging into the side of her head. She was trying to be brave, but her eyes were wide and dark in fear. My stomach turned, bile rising in my throat. I had to think. Had to focus. There was a way to get out of this. Even if it meant sacrificing myself, I would never let him have her. As I looked up to meet Brenner's eyes, I showed him every ounce of my hatred.

He laughed. "Well, Valentine, I'll give you credit for this much: you've certainly managed to surprise me. My soldiers told me it would have been impossible for anyone to survive that crash, and yet here you are. Moreover, you show no signs whatsoever of having been infected by my parasite."

I kept silent, waiting for even the slimmest opportunity. If there was one thing of which I was certain, it was that Brenner loved the sound of his own voice. The longer he talked at us, the longer we had to think of something.

"So what I'm wondering, Valentine," he continued, "is exactly how much you would give me to spare your girlfriend's life. I'm still going to give her to my soldiers, of course. I'd already promised you that, and I don't break my promises. But they won't kill her, whereas I have no compunctions whatsoever about embedding one of these slugs into—"

A black blur. The flash of light reflecting from curved teeth. Reality slowed as Constantine appeared from behind the cover of the nearest cubicle, leaping directly for the throat of his nemesis.

Instinctively, Brenner shifted his weapon away from Alexa and fired into the panther's mouth. Alexa dove for one of my guns as I stretched for the other. Gunfire filled the air, and Brenner's body jerked wildly as he was riddled with bullets.

I couldn't stop pulling the trigger. My weapon clicked hollowly, having long since run out of ammunition, but I couldn't stop. I couldn't stop.

Alexa's trembling hand closed over mine. She stilled my trigger finger, then slid the gun out of my grasp. Beyond words, I crushed her to me.

"Did he hurt you at all?" I finally managed to ask.

She exhaled shakily. "No. Thanks to Constantine."

She buried her face in the crook of my neck, and I rubbed my cheek against her hair, exulting in the feel and scent of her. Warm. Alive. Mine. As the horror of seeing her in Brenner's clutches began gradually to subside, I realized just how dear a price we had paid for Brenner's death. Constantine Bellande, who—like Alexa—had become a wereshifter in order to save a family member, had died the way he lived: sacrificing himself for others.

Karma and Malcolm were standing over his body, their heads bowed. "He died a hero," Malcolm said, voice rough with unshed tears. "But we have no time to grieve for him now." He lifted Constantine's bloodied corpse, cradling him in his arms. "We have to hurry."

As we jogged through the corridors, we formed a phalanx around him—Foster and Karma in front, Alexa and me behind. Our search for a staircase led us into one small group of guards, but we were able to dispatch them quickly.

When we finally emerged into open air, I let the tears run freely down my cheeks, unashamed. Brenner was dead, his reign of terror over. As Malcolm called for the chopper that would extract us to safety, I wrapped my arms around Alexa. Together, we grieved for the man who had saved us in so many ways.

By siring Alexa, Constantine had allowed her to become a wereshifter when no one else would. He had made it possible for her to save my soul—not once, but twice.

We owed him more than our lives, and we would spend the rest of eternity in his debt.

EPILOGUE

The white oak conference table made a graceful U-shape in the middle of the Consortium's newly renovated meeting hall. After Brenner's sacking of Headquarters, an executive decision had been made to remodel the facility with an all new design that favored wide-open spaces over starkly delineated offices. The new conference room was emblematic of the new regime: a practical and comfortable gathering space that was equipped to accommodate vampires and wereshifters equally. Underneath the table, Alexa's hand rested warmly against my thigh. I leaned my shoulder into hers and luxuriated in her nearness.

Malcolm and Foster stood side by side at the mouth of the U, while satellite photos flashed on the screen behind them. Helen and Solana occupied the far corner. So far they had been mostly quiet, letting Malcolm and Foster run the meeting. It was highly uncharacteristic of Helen to be so laissez-faire in such a high profile gathering. Then again, in the past, most of those meetings had been held behind closed doors with just a small handful of trusted lieutenants present. During those meetings, Helen had barked commands and the rest of us heeded them.

Today, every seat in the room was filled and several more observers stood against the back wall. Vampires and shifters were present in equal numbers. I had been surprised to find Sebastian among the invited. He had given me the cold shoulder as I made eye contact. He still hadn't forgiven me for sniping him—or for divorcing him, for that matter—but I wasn't bothered. We had eternity to make up.

Malcolm rested his hand on a thick binder on the table in front of him. "We've managed to secure thousands of files and hard drives from Brenner's research facility. Our data teams in India and New Zealand are going through them now to see if anything is usable. Early reports have identified pockets of shifter rebel camps in Outer Mongolia. Beijing headquarters has been notified and will be sending reconnaissance soon."

Foster flipped to a grainy aerial shot of a cloud of smoke blanketing a densely wooded area. "We've scavenged Brenner's equipment and requisitioned usable weapons and laboratory equipment. The rest of the facility will be dismantled and demolished within the next six to eight weeks."

I raised my hand and waited for Foster's acknowledgement. "The hybrid parasite?"

Foster pulled a small notepad from her breast pocket and flipped through it. "We found notes indicating that Brenner was synthesizing an injectable version of the parasite and was planning on distributing it through his underground drug network."

"Christopher Blaine's network now," Alexa pointed out. "Who shows every sign of filling the power vacuum left by his father. On the human end of things, at any rate."

"I have Olivia Lloyd investigating the drug connection," I added. "Can we pass on additional leads to her?"

In the short time we'd been away, Olivia had already begun making inroads into Blaine's operation. She was working undercover and had reported success at infiltrating the circle of a low-level dealer while simultaneously passing tips along to the police.

Foster nodded. "We have some org charts and some maps that might be useful to Olivia. I'll be sure to send them along."

I leaned back in my chair, satisfied that she would continue to sniff out Blaine's underhanded dealings. As both Alexa and I knew, Olivia in bloodhound mode was relentless. And in the meanwhile, her investigation had had its desired effect. The regulatory attacks on my bank had completely stopped while Blaine dealt not only with the fallout of Olivia's efforts, but of our assassination of his father.

The slide on the screen changed to a satellite photo over Africa. Malcolm stepped forward and Foster surrendered her laser pointer to him. "Scouting forces have captured the last of the Telassar raiders. We've secured the compound and installed a defense force onsite as well as reinforced the armed personnel at the nearest outposts." Malcolm flipped to a new image and used a laser pointer to highlight the reinforcements.

"Communications systems?" Helen's voice was soft but steady. It was her first question of the meeting.

"Negative. We've decided to maintain the technological blackout at Telassar. Instead, we have implemented a patrol and check-in system that increases the participation of the outposts and guards in communicating the situation in the keep."

Helen nodded solemnly. "Constantine would have wanted it that way."

Malcolm dipped his head in acknowledgement. "We have pushed the boundaries of our secrecy with the recent infiltration of the Four Seasons and Brenner's attack on Consortium Headquarters. It has taken all of our political capital and then some to cover up our actions. It seemed prudent to fly under the radar as much as possible in all manners of our operations."

"Thank you both for the update," she said. "Is that all?"

"Actually…" Malcolm hesitated and glanced at Karma. "I've decided to step down as Weremaster of New York City. Instead, I would like to oversee the reconstruction of Telassar."

A collective gasp and mumbling erupted throughout the room. I turned to Alexa and saw that she was as shocked as I. Simultaneously, we both turned toward Karma who sat calmly and with great poise. I managed to catch her eye and she smiled so slightly I barely caught it. Damn it, she had known. Beside me, Alexa growled subvocally. Neither of us liked to be kept in the dark.

Helen showed neither surprise nor alarm. "When will you be leaving?"

"Next week. I have already begun transferring my responsibilities to Karma and I plan on making frequent trips back to New York until the leadership transition is complete."

Helen turned her steel gray gaze toward Karma. "Ms. Rao will be your successor, then?"

Karma smiled, the effect of Helen's scrutiny making as little impact as BBs against Kevlar. "We'll be forming a Were-council to make executive decisions. Eventually, we hope to have half a dozen council members, but for now, we will start with three. I will be serving on the council alongside Alexa Newland and Sebastian Brenner."

Alexa's hand jerked on my thigh and Sebastian, who had been leaning back in his chair throughout the meeting, came crashing down with a string of muffled obscenities. Even Helen gave a start at the proclamation. Helen glanced at Malcolm who stood silent and intractable at the head of the room.

Silence stretched for long seconds before Helen finally turned her attention back to Karma. "I look forward to working with your council."

I wondered how hard that sentence had been to spit out. Helen wasn't exactly known for espousing any kind of democratic process.

"If there is nothing more?" When no one spoke, she nodded once. "Then we will reconvene in a week's time."

Solana stood first and helped Helen to her feet and then toward the door. One by one, the members of the meeting followed suit. I saw Sebastian make a beeline for Karma. Alexa, I could tell, wanted to do the same, but she was waiting on me. "Go ahead, love, I'll catch up with you later. I'd like to talk with Helen."

Alexa leaned in and kissed me and then hurried after Karma and Sebastian. I exited the conference room, jogged down the hallway, and caught up with Helen and Solana at the elevator bank.

I smiled at them both, but let my gaze linger on Helen. She was wearing lighter bandages on her face and hands and her limp was almost gone.

"How are you?"

"Harold tells me that my recovery is proceeding as scheduled." Helen's right hand was tucked gently in Solana's arm. The elevator arrived and we stepped inside together.

"Good. I'm glad to hear it." I swiped my ID badge against the scanner and punched in the floor where my new research facility was being built.

"How is your lab coming along?" Solana keyed the floor for Helen's private residence. "Do you need me to stop by again to provide more samples?"

"The equipment is almost all in. Brenner was very extravagant in his research. I'm grateful for his generous, albeit posthumous, donation to our cause."

Solana laughed and I joined her. This sense of optimism still felt so new.

"I'm set with samples for now, but we'll probably want to run some more tests in a month. How are you feeling?"

"Good. Great. I took the flower extract yesterday, as soon as it arrived from Argentina. I think I probably could have gone several more weeks without it, but I didn't want to risk it."

The elevator dinged as we arrived at my floor. I stepped out but held the door open. "I don't want to jinx anything, but all the tests on the flower thus far seem promising. I have a briefing set with Clavier next week to finalize the next step in our research plan."

Helen reached out and grasped my forearm. "Well done, Valentine. I'll look forward to Harold's report."

I stepped back and let the elevator door close, reflecting on just how much my life had changed over the past two years. Then, I had been a medical student. Now, I commanded a medical lab. Then, I had never fired a gun. Now, I was one of the best marksmen in the Consortium. Then, I had believed vampires and shifters to be fantastical—if entertaining—stories. Now, I counted many vampires and shifters to be closer to me than my blood relations.

Then, I had been on the verge of proposing to the love of my life. Now…a smile formed on my lips and I turned toward my office to wait for Alexa.

❖

She didn't arrive for over an hour, and as soon as I opened the door, she dragged me over to the couch beneath the window. The sun had risen moments ago, and its new light played across the glossy leather.

"How did everything go, Councilwoman?" I asked, leaning back against one armrest and pulling her into the space between my legs. "Is that what I'm supposed to call you now?"

She tilted her head back and glared at me. "Don't make fun."

"No? All right then, I'll make fun of Sebastian. How's he taking the news?"

Alexa laughed. "Oh, he hates it. It's responsibility."

"Make him do everything," I said. "I mean it: everything."

We sat in silence for a while, simply enjoying each other's company. I gently stroked her arms and she occupied herself by kissing my neck. But after a while I felt her withdraw, and I knew she was thinking of Constantine.

"How are *you* doing, sweetheart?"

"It hurts," she said after a moment. "It hasn't stopped hurting and it probably never will."

I took my time in replying, choosing my words carefully. "You know I never want to see you in pain. But maybe this kind of hurt is…okay. Constantine was like a father to you. I don't think something like that is ever supposed to stop being painful."

She nodded against my chest. "I'm glad Malcolm is going over to Telassar. He's the perfect person to carry on Constantine's legacy."

"Well, besides you."

"I'm only related by blood. In many ways, I think Malcolm's better suited for it. Ever since he came back from being feral, he's had really profound insights into the animal psyche. He'll serve Telassar well."

I stared out at the lightening sky, wondering if now was really the right time for what I'd planned.

"Aside from Constantine," I said carefully, "is there anything else on your mind?"

She turned in my embrace and threaded her arms around my neck. "No, not at all. Aside from that, I'm happy. Relieved. Cautiously optimistic."

I kissed her neck, then gently moved her forward so I could stand. "That exact word popped into my head earlier," I said as I went to my desk and opened the top drawer.

I looked up to find her watching me—not because she was curious about what was I doing, but because she loved me. No matter where I was in the room, her eyes followed me. I did the very same when it came to her.

I withdrew a small piece of paper and held it out before me as I crossed back to her. She took it from me with a quizzical look, then bent her head to read it.

"I want you to have this," I said into the silence. "I want us to have this."

"The deed to that cabin?" Her eyes glowed with happiness as she looked up at me, and I could practically hear her inner panther purring. "And the surrounding one hundred acres?"

"Well, I thought your other self might enjoy some space for hunting."

When she smiled at me in childlike anticipation, I had to return the expression.

"Are you serious?"

"So serious," I said, "that I want you to go there with me. Right now."

The next moment, she was in my arms.

❖

The first signs of spring—the occasional budding tree and intrepid crocus—had arrived in Manhattan. But up here in the Catskills, winter still wrapped the land in frozen bonds, and I was glad of the metal spikes on the undersides of my snowshoes. The trail wound between trees whose branches seemed to have been dipped into frosting. On a whim, I stopped and tasted the snow cradled by a nearby pine. Cold and pure, it dissolved instantaneously on my tongue, momentarily eclipsing the fire of my ever-present thirst. When a breeze rattled the evergreen treetops, the thick canopy parted enough for me to see the sky. Its subtle mocha hue foreshadowed the sunrise a scant half an hour away. I needed to keep moving if I was going to make the summit in time.

Reflexively, I felt for the small bundle in my right pocket as I continued along the trail. Common sense told me that I'd zipped up that pocket back at the trailhead and hadn't touched it since, but until this plan had been executed to perfection, I knew I'd keep checking. Alexa and I had arrived last night to find "our" cabin virtually unchanged since the last time we'd been here two years ago. Back then, Alexa had still been struggling to find equilibrium with her panther, and this had been the place where we'd finally made a breakthrough. The cabin represented the strength of our relationship in the face of all obstacles, and it was the perfect place for us to rest and recharge after the grueling months we'd just endured.

We were both exhausted from dealing with the fallout of Brenner's schemes, and Alexa hadn't been all that keen on the idea of waking up at four o'clock in the morning for a chance to watch the sunrise from the mountaintop. She had groaned and grumbled, delivering ominous ultimatums about how I'd have to make this up to her. But once on the trail, the contentment of her feline half trumped any residual annoyance. Now she was off somewhere in the forest, indulging her panther's desire to hunt.

The trees began to thin out as trail became even steeper. After a series of switchbacks, I emerged onto a long curving ridge ascending to the summit. As I walked along the exposed spine of the mountain, I watched the stars gradually fade from view. A hush had settled over the world, as though the rocks and trees were taking a long, deep breath in preparation for the day ahead. Even up here, the air was still.

One last, steep ascent stood between me and the stone cairn that marked the mountain's highest point. I had just begun the climb when a sudden blur of motion stopped me in my tracks, and instinctively I fell into a defensive crouch. But as quickly as it had come, the spike of adrenaline faded and a smile tugged at my lips.

Never taking my eyes off the large black cat that now crouched upon the pile of rocks, I rose to my full height and continued my approach.

As a woman, Alexa inspired in me a passion laced with love, admiration, and respect. As a panther, she commanded my deference. The coiled strength of her haunches, the volatile twitches of her thick tail, the deadly elegance of her curved teeth—she was a living weapon in ways I could never be. Together, we were the perfect team. Now more than ever.

I stopped in front of the cairn. "You can be Queen of the Mountain. Really. I won't fight you for it."

Her eyes squinted in that characteristic feline smile, and a low purr rumbled from her throat. When I set down my backpack and pulled out her clothes, she leapt from the rocks to land soundlessly at my feet and butted her head against my legs. I lost my balance and stumbled backward, laughing.

"You're not exactly a housecat, baby."

Crouching, I stroked the silky fur behind her ears and dared to meet her unblinking gaze. Face to face with her like this, it was so easy to understand why Egyptians had worshipped their cats.

"You're beautiful. But the sun is about to rise, and I'd like to give you a proper kiss when it does. What do you think?"

Immediately, the air began to shimmer, and I stepped back to give her some room. When she appeared, naked and kneeling before me, I swallowed against the hot flare of thirst that parched my throat. Her pale skin glowed in the fading starlight and my hands ached to touch her, but I balled them into fists. Right now, I had a different priority. I needed to stay focused.

"Hi."

"Hi." As she stood and reached for the clothes, her smile was just the tiniest bit smug. "Thanks for carrying these up."

I glanced to the east, where the sky was brightest. Still some time, but not much. Now that Alexa was back in human form I found myself oddly nervous. Maybe if I kept her talking, she wouldn't notice.

"How was your hunt?"

"Beautiful." She paused to slide her shirt over her head. "I saw a bear. He reminded me a little of Delacourte. You never got to meet him. He died during our escape from Brenner in Africa. But he was a good friend in Telassar."

The note of sorrow in her voice tore at me. "Brenner has so much blood on his hands. Sometimes death seems too kind for him."

"I'm glad he's gone. It's a relief not to have to worry about him anymore."

Once she had zipped up her jacket, I pulled her close. "You have too much on your mind already, Councilwoman."

"Don't you dare," she said, sliding her arms around my neck. "Up here, I'm no one's councilwoman."

Our combined breaths steamed into the air between us, mingling and rising. But when she leaned in, I pulled back.

"Wait. Let's watch the sunrise." I spun her in my arms and turned us both to face east, but she refused to go quietly.

"Who are you and what have you done with Valentine?" Twisting in my embrace, she frowned at me. "I think that may be the first time you've ever rejected an attempt of mine to kiss you."

"Believe me, I want very badly to kiss you. I just want to wait a few more minutes until I can do it in the sunlight."

Alexa's expression softened and she drew my arms more tightly around her. Together, we watched as a subtle golden glow began to spread over the dark mountaintops. Gradually, the light expanded, blanketing the surrounding peaks, and I struggled not to shade my eyes against the growing brightness at its core.

And then, finally, the sun broke free. Orange rays of light advanced across the forested slopes to pierce the valley, illuminating the frozen river below. Prisms danced in the air beneath us as the light was scattered by snow and ice. I pulled Alexa even closer.

"How does it feel, knowing you make it possible for me to be standing here?"

This time I didn't stop her when she turned. Her eyes glistened with emotion as she caressed my cheek. And as I stood there on top of the world, bathed in new light, looking down at the woman who had saved not only my life and my heart but also my soul, I knew the time was finally right.

I stepped back just far enough to drop to one knee. Somehow, I managed to unzip the pocket and reach inside without ever breaking Alexa's gaze. The light played across her expressive features, illuminating her surprise, her happiness, her love. For me. Taking a deep breath, I pulled out the small black box that I'd been keeping in reserve for years now.

"The night when I was turned, I was planning to give you this. I wanted to marry you, and then everything changed. My world has turned upside down in so many ways since then, but you've always been there to show me which way is up."

When she opened her mouth to speak, I swallowed hard and held up one finger. I wasn't finished.

"In an eternity of days, more than a few will likely become chaotic. But no matter what happens next, I want to be bound to you in every way possible. Forever—literally. So, Alexa Newland, will you marry me?"

Joy burst over her face, a second sunrise. I basked in it, taking a mental snapshot of the way she looked right now: emerald eyes gleaming, cheeks brightly flushed, lips parted in advance of her answer.

"Yes."

She reached down and pulled me to my feet, then flung her arms around my neck and sealed her promise with a long, slow kiss. Already dizzy with happiness, I willingly lost myself in the sensation of her lips moving against mine.

Finally, she leaned back in my arms just far enough to look into my eyes.

"I love you, Valentine. The woman you were then, and are now. I love you. My answer will always be yes."

About the Authors

Nell Stark is an Assistant Professor of English and the Director of the Writing Center at a college in the SUNY system. Trinity Tam is a marketing executive in the music industry and an award-winning writer/producer of film and television. They live, write, and parent a rambunctious toddler just a stone's throw from the historic Stonewall Inn in New York City. For more information about the everafter series, visit www.everafterseries.com.

Books Available from Bold Strokes Books

Dark Wings Descending by Lesley Davis. What if the demons you face in life are real? Chicago detective Rafe Douglas is about to find out. (978-1-60282-660-1)

sunfall by Nell Stark and Trinity Tam. The final installment of the everafter series. Valentine Darrow and Alexa Newland work to rebuild their relationship even as they find themselves at the heart of the struggle that will determine a new world order for vampires and wereshifters. (978-1-60282-661-8)

Mission of Desire by Terri Richards. Nicole Kennedy finds herself in Africa at the center of an international conspiracy and being rescued by beautiful but arrogant government agent Kira Anthony, but is Kira someone Nicole can trust or is she blinded by desire? (978-1-60282-662-5)

Boys of Summer edited by Steve Berman. Stories of young love and adventure, when the sky's ceiling is a bright blue marvel, when another boy's laughter at the beach can distract from dull summer jobs. (978-1-60282-663-2)

The Locket and the Flintlock by Rebecca S. Buck. When Regency gentlewoman Lucia Foxe is robbed on the highway, will the masked outlaw who stole Lucia's precious locket also claim her heart? (978-1-60282-664-9)

Calendar Boys by Zachary Logan. A man a month will keep you excited year round. (978-1-60282-665-6)

Burgundy Betrayal by Sheri Lewis Wohl. Park Ranger Kara Lynch has no idea she's a witch until dead bodies begin to pile up in her park, forcing her to turn to beautiful and sexy shape-shifter Camille Black Wolf for help in stopping a rogue werewolf. (978-1-60282-654-0)

LoveLife by Rachel Spangler. When Joey Lang unintentionally becomes a client of life coach Elaine Raitt, the relationship becomes complicated as they develop feelings that make them question their purpose in love and life. (978-1-60282-655-7)

The Fling by Rebekah Weatherspoon. When the ultimate fantasy of a one-night stand with her trainer, Oksana Gorinkov, suddenly turns into more, reality show producer Annie Collins opens her life to a new type of love she's never imagined. (978-1-60282-656-4)

Ill Will by J.M. Redmann. New Orleans PI Micky Knight must untangle a twisted web of healthcare fraud that leads to murder—and puts those closest to her most at risk. (978-1-60282-657-1)

Buccaneer Island by J.P. Beausejour. In the rough world of Caribbean piracy, a man is what he makes of himself—or what a stronger man makes of him. (978-1-60282-658-8)

Twelve O'Clock Tales by Felice Picano. The fourth collection of short fiction by legendary novelist and memoirist Felice Picano. Thirteen dark tales that will thrill and disturb, discomfort and titillate, enthrall and leave you wondering. (978-1-60282-659-5)

Words to Die By by William Holden. Sixteen answers to the question: What causes a mind to curdle? (978-1-60282-653-3)

Tyger, Tyger, Burning Bright by Justine Saracen. Love does not conquer all, but when all of Europe is on fire, it's better than going to hell alone. (978-1-60282-652-6)

Night Hunt by L.L. Raand. When dormant powers ignite, the wolf Were pack is thrown into violent upheaval, and Sylvan's pregnant mate is at the center of the turmoil. A Midnight Hunters novel. (978-1-60282-647-2)

Demons are Forever by Kim Baldwin and Xenia Alexiou. Elite Operative Landis "Chase" Coolidge enlists the help of high-class call girl Heather Snyder to track down a kidnapped colleague embroiled in a global black market organ-harvesting ring. (978-1-60282-648-9)

Runaway by Anne Laughlin. When Jan Roberts is hired to find a teenager who has run away to live with a group of antigovernment survivalists, she's forced to return to the life she escaped when she was a teenager herself. (978-1-60282-649-6)

Street Dreams by Tama Wise. Tyson Rua has more than his fair share of problems growing up in New Zealand—he's gay, he's falling in love, and he's run afoul of the local hip-hop crew leader just as he's trying to make it as a graffiti artist. (978-1-60282-650-2)

Women of the Dark Streets: Lesbian Paranormal by Radclyffe and Stacia Seaman, eds. Erotic tales of the supernatural—a world of vampires, werewolves, witches, ghosts, and demons—by the authors of Bold Strokes Books. (978-1-60282-651-9)